NEW YEAR KISS
WITH HIS CINDERELLA

———

ANNIE O'NEIL

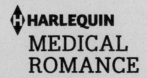

MEDICAL
ROMANCE

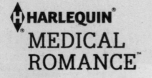

HARLEQUIN®
MEDICAL
ROMANCE™

Recycling programs
for this product may
not exist in your area.

ISBN-13: 978-1-335-40899-0

New Year Kiss with His Cinderella

Harlequin Enterprises ULC
22 Adelaide St. West, 41st Floor
Toronto, Ontario M5H 4E3, Canada
www.Harlequin.com

Printed in U.S.A.

Nashville ER

Saving lives and healing hearts!

After a busy shift at Nashville's
Saint Dolores Hospital, aka St. Dolly's,
Avery Whittacker and Lia Costa love nothing
more than meeting up for gossip, guacamole and a
pitcher of margaritas. The friends agree on almost
everything, including that neither has room in her
life for romance...

But the New Year brings two new doctors to their
busy ER, who make waves in the department and
set the friends' hearts fluttering!

Nurse practitioner Avery Whittacker isn't
looking for love, until one of St. Dolly's
newest MDs, Carter Booth, gets under her skin
and into her heart, in:

New Year Kiss with His Cinderella
By Annie O'Neil

Vascular surgeon Lia Costa is perfectly happy
focusing on her career, until Dr. Micah Corday
comes back into her life—a decade after she broke
both their hearts by sending him away, in:

Their Reunion to Remember
By Tina Beckett

Dear Reader,

Hello there! Get yer cowboy boots ready because we're going to Nashville!

When Tina and I were given the thumbs-up on our idea for this Tennessee-set duet, we were over the moon. I had just finished watching the series *Nashville* and was obsessed! There's something about a town dedicated to making music that makes your heart sing as well.

I hope you enjoy Carter and Avery's story. I certainly had a wonderful time writing it.

Please do reach out on social media. You can find me @annieoneilbooks on Twitter or Instagram.

xx *Annie O'*

Annie O'Neil spent most of her childhood with her leg draped over the family rocking chair and a book in her hand. Reading, baking and writing too much teenage-angst poetry ate up most of her youth. Now Annie splits her time between corralling her husband into helping her with their cows, baking, reading, barrel racing (not really!) and spending some very happy hours at her computer writing.

Books by Annie O'Neil

Harlequin Medical Romance

The Island Clinic
The Princess and the Pediatrician

Double Miracle at St. Nicolino's Hospital
A Family Made in Rome

Dolphin Cove Vets
The Vet's Secret Son

Miracles in the Making
Risking Her Heart on the Single Dad

Christmas Under the Northern Lights
Hawaiian Medic to Rescue His Heart

Visit the Author Profile page
at Harlequin.com for more titles.

This one is for and with gratitude to the wonderful
Tina Beckett, who made this *such* fun to write.
I am deeply jealous of her upcoming
trip to Dollywood.

Praise for
Annie O'Neil

"With her poignant way of wrapping a character
around her reader's heart, Annie O'Neil does it
once again in *Risking Her Heart on the Single Dad*.
The emotion is high throughout the story, and
the characters are well developed and inspiring. I
highly recommend this book to anyone who loves
a medical romance filled with emotion and heart."
—*Goodreads*

CHAPTER ONE

CARTER LET OUT a low satisfied whistle. He'd never seen a woman ride a mechanical bull like she was doing a ballet before. Some kind of dance anyway. She was undulating with the erratic whips and spins of the longhorn as if she could predict it. Not jerking around like her predecessors, most of whom, courtesy of too much tequila, had been flung onto the mats within seconds.

Not this woman. Her right arm was up in the air, hand cupped like she was royalty, her left wrapped around the leather-bound handhold as if she were idly steering a shopping cart with wheels that worked. That made her a leftie, then. Like him. A confident one.

She had a gorgeous billow of hair blowing in the light wintry breeze, snowflakes catching in it like they were diamonds. Skin the color of coffee with the perfect dollop of cream in it.

Sexy as hell is what she was. Sexy enough to require a shift to his belt buckle at least.

Her dark eyes were lit up by the myriad of neon lights vying for competition out here in the heart of Nashville's party street. Honky Tonk Row. Everything blinked and glowed at maximum party levels. He guessed tonight was a party for most folk. New Year's Eve wasn't anything special to him. Just another day. A busy one if he were at work. But that didn't start until tomorrow. First day of another New Year in another new town. One he might actually learn the street grid for this time. Maybe.

If this woman were a sign of things to come, maybe Nashville wouldn't be so bad after all.

She wasn't smiling, but her lips weren't pressed into a thin line of grim determination, either. They were pushed forward in a thoughtful pout. Fancy people would probably call it a *moue*. But fancy was the last thing he was.

He reckoned this was her thinking face. He liked it. Could easily imagine cupping her jawline in his hands, stroking his thumb along her cheek and pulling her to him to turn her expression into something that looked a lot more like a smile. He let his gaze shift down past the sheepskin collar buttoned up close around her neck, beyond the flannel-lined jean jacket and slide down those long legs of hers, also clad in denim. They were holding onto the hide covered "bull" as if they genuinely wanted to. Not like most folk did—for dear life. He laughed. She knew she was good. That she was going to win the cash prize. Upward of two thousand dollars now and growing by the minute. The more takers, the bigger the pot.

And then she looked at him.

He felt it at once. The connection. A carnal one that lit him up like electricity, heating every primitive cell in his body quicker than fire.

Carter's lips curved into the first happy smile they'd made since he'd arrived here in Nashville. Next thing he knew, the mechanical longhorn was flinging her to the mat, landing her at his feet.

When he reached down to help pull her up, it was like trying to hold onto a wildcat. She was raging. Not in a screaming, angry way. In a low deliberate way that for some reason made him want to pull her into his arms and direct all that energy into something a bit more...not productive exactly.

"Thanks for nothing," she growled.

"Hey." He body-blocked a couple of drunken twenty-somethings trying to push their way into the cordoned off ring around the bull, his gaze never leaving hers. "I was just standing here, minding my own business."

"Ruining my chances of walking away with the cash is what you were doing,"

"Is that what the goal was?"

Something flickered through her defiant expression. A vulnerability. One she instantly hid with a jutted chin and a slight curl to her top lip. She'd betrayed too much to him and was regretting it.

They both looked at the leaderboard. She was ahead of the previous riders by ten seconds. He could tell by the look on her face she'd been hoping to secure that lead by something much more substantial.

"You need that money?" he asked.

It was bold. Putting it out there like that. No one liked their pride dented, but he wasn't one to step away from a bit of straight talking. Most of the time anyway. He crossed his arms and waited. He'd seen what she was made of physically and mentally atop that bull. Now it was time to see what sort of emotional grit held her together.

"I don't recall informing you that it was any of your business." There was a smile on her face, but it wasn't a warm one.

Okay. Good. He got it. No one said laying your cards on the table was a smart thing to do. Especially with a stranger. Even so, he could see they both knew her answer meant yes. She needed the money and blamed him for cracking that laser sharp concentration of hers that had all but guaranteed a bulging wallet come midnight.

"I'll win it for you," he said.

She laughed. "Yeah, right." Her dark brown eyes flicked up to his Stetson. "This isn't the state fair, cowboy. I don't need a stuffed toy."

Shame. It was pretty easy to picture the two of them walking through a fun fair. Him with a deep-fried pickle—yeah, it was a thing—and her with a huge old teddy bear balanced on that curvy hip of hers. He tipped his head toward the line of people waiting their turn to ride the bull before the clock struck midnight. He gave his chest a thump with a fist. "Nothing but blood and bones in this prize. Carter Booth, at your service." He took off his hat and bowed.

When he rose, her arms were crossed, and her expression had shifted from irritated to something trickier to read. He reckoned he had about a sixty-second window to win her over.

He had some height on her, but somehow she was smiling down her nose at him even though her chin was practically vertical. Nice trick. It could definitely put someone on edge. Not him. But somebody.

"If you actually could ride longer than me, it'd be your money you'd be winning." She didn't tell him her name. But the comment told him a lot about her character.

"No." That wasn't how he saw it. "I wasn't planning on riding tonight, and I'm guessing you would've been up there a while longer if my good looks hadn't thrown you off balance."

She made a noise of protest. And this time, she definitely blushed. He knew he wasn't a pretty boy. More rough than ready. But his gut was telling him she liked the look of whatever it was he had going for him and, for tonight at least, that was good enough for him.

Her eyes narrowed. "What do you want in return?"

"A kiss."

Well, what do you know? He hadn't known he was in possession of that much temerity. His brain threw him back to the moment he'd told his last boss to stuff it. Then again, maybe he did.

Her eyebrows were raised almost up to her forehead. "What? On the cheek?"

He shook his head and tapped a finger on his lips, enjoying himself that little bit more when he saw her fight a shiver of anticipation. "Stroke of midnight," he continued. "Then just like Cinderella, I'll disappear out of your life."

She laughed out loud at this. "I thought that was my role."

He shrugged. "You can be the princess. I've never been one to kowtow to the so-called patriarchy." He believed in a lot of things. Democracy. Freedom. Looking after the people you loved. Especially family. Respect. Honesty. When it was required. He also believed in moving in and out of town without setting down roots because, as sure as the seasons would change, his sister would be doing something that meant he'd have to throw his duffel bags and guitar in the back of his truck and hit the road again.

"You're that confident, are you?" she asked, her tongue dipping out for a quick swipe along her lips.

She was warming to him. Good.

The guy who'd climbed on the bull after her had been thrown off and someone else was climbing on. Carter would glue himself to the bull if that's what it took to stay on the longest. But it wouldn't take that. Back in Texas, he'd called his riding paying the bills. His sister had called it sheer stupidity. They'd both been right.

"Never met a bull who didn't take to my winning personality." He tipped the brim of his hat to her.

Her eyes didn't leave his. "If you win my money, I'm not taking it."

"And I'm not letting you walk away empty-handed."

She frowned. "I guess you'd better come up with something else, then. I don't steal prizes that aren't mine."

He held his hands out, then ran them alongside his body. "Apart from my guitar, this is the only other thing I've got on offer."

He wasn't actually broke. He wasn't a thief, either. That role in the family was already taken.

A loud roar from the crowd filled the air as another contender climbed aboard the longhorn.

She tilted her head to the side, and he took the few moments she was assessing him to do the same. Skin that looked so soft there probably wasn't a thread count high enough for it. A body that rocked the hell out of her double-denim getup. A pair of cowboy boots that definitely weren't just for show. God*damn* she was sexy.

"Well, then," she said. "I guess you'd better get on up there and show me what you got." When she met his gaze, he was pretty sure he wasn't only seeing neon lights flaring in her eyes.

She put out her mittened hand. They were going to shake on it, apparently.

Carter smiled. Progress. She liked him, too. Enough to want to see him show his stuff atop a mechanical bull anyway. Maybe she merely wanted a good laugh. Either way, he could work with that. Not that he'd be seeing her again, but…it was New Year's Eve. The bit of him that believed in destiny, that hoped that fate wasn't something only poets spoke of, wanted her appearance in his life to signify something more than a chance meeting. Yet another moment in time that would slip through his fingers when reality reared its head and cut things short. Again.

It surprised him how much he wanted her to be a sign of good things to come. Needed it, even. Perhaps if he won that kiss…

He put his thumb and index finger on the tip of her thumb. "May I?"

She didn't say anything, but she didn't refuse. Just watched, mesmerized, as he tugged off her mitten, slowly, so that when their hands finally met, it would be flesh on flesh.

The atmosphere changed. The sounds of the crowd dulled and somehow, the way the world can sometimes, everything stilled so that it seemed like it was just the two of them out here in the middle of Nashville with nothing but a few flakes of snow between them.

When he finally cupped her hand in his, her

eyes widened. A sound escaped her throat. One that gave the impression she'd just been touched somewhere much more intimate than her palm. And that she liked it. He barely managed to stop a guttural exhalation from escaping his own throat. It pleased him that she felt the connection, too. It'd been a while since he'd pulled out his flirtation skills and chances were they were real rusty.

"Avery!"

She pulled her hand away, turning toward the sound of the woman's voice. He saw a tall slender dark-haired woman waving in their direction. She was beautiful, too, but didn't catch his eye in quite the same way the one in front of him did.

This woman—"his" woman—waved. "Over here, Lia."

Okay. First mystery solved. Her name was Avery. Nice. It tasted good. He liked the way his teeth had to scrape against his bottom lip to say it. Now all he had to do was figure out if this Lia was her friend, her wingman or both.

"Hey, Avery." Lia, bundled up to her chin in a thick winter parka, hip-bumped her friend. "Who's this?"

They both turned to look at Carter.

Avery shrugged. "He claims he's my knight

in shining armor." They shared a complicit look. "Don't worry. Not worth remembering."

As if the words were some secret code, the two of them started giggling.

"I think you'll find otherwise," Carter said. "I'm going to win that money."

"What money?" she riposted. "You mean my money?"

They looked at the leaderboard and though only a few seconds stood between her and the last rider, she was still in pole position.

Lia's smile dropped away. She lowered her voice and asked Avery something he couldn't quite catch with all the hullabaloo around them. Another joker climbed on board the longhorn. Lia and Avery were sharing a look that spoke to him loud and clear. She'd genuinely been banking on that cash.

The guy fell off in about three seconds flat. Another contender clambered up. A woman who fell off the second they set the bull in motion and was whisked away by a group of friends.

He glanced at the clock. Time was running short.

"If you'll excuse me, ladies." He tipped his hat to Lia first, then Avery with whom he held eye contact. "I'm off to win my kiss."

Avery, clearly emboldened by her friend's

arrival threw him a wicked smile. "I don't recall giving you permission to have that kiss."

"Well, we'll see about that. Here, keep an eye on this for me, would you? I presume you're trustworthy enough not to make off with a man's guitar?"

Avery nodded, her eyes fleetingly taking on a look of longing as they set on his guitar case.

Five minutes later, the crowd was counting down to midnight and Avery's name was still ahead on the leaderboard. She hadn't cold-shouldered him after he'd fallen off two seconds short of her time, but her focus had definitely narrowed in on the bar owner who was poised to hand out the prize—now double what it had been twenty minutes ago when he'd first seen her.

Once she had the envelope safely tucked inside her jacket, he was surprised to find her standing in front of him as the counting hit the single digits. Fewer than five seconds to go and it would be a New Year. Three. Two. And then they were kissing.

He didn't need fireworks to feel lit up inside. The touch of her lips, warm and soft and interested in exploring his was all the heat he needed. If he hadn't been holding a guitar in one hand, he'd have hooked her legs up and around his hips faster than she could've blinked. Carried her back to his soulless serviced apartment and spent the rest of the night setting her on fire. He heard a hint of a moan as he drew his thumb down her throat to her collarbone. The sort that meant he'd give his right arm to elicit a proper one.

She pulled back first.

He shifted his stance. Had to. His jeans were officially uncomfortable. In the drollest voice he had, he said, "Well, that was unexpected." It was a massive understatement. "I feel like I collected on something I didn't earn."

She considered him for a moment, running her index finger along those lips of hers. Fuller now that they were bruised from kissing. "Well, I guess you owe me, then." She smiled, turned, then walked away. Before he could get his brain working straight, she'd disappeared into the crowd.

He smiled. Laughed to himself. It had been a risk to fall off the bull early, but something had told him she wouldn't have taken the money if he'd grandstanded in front of her. And he'd still got his kiss. All in all, it was a good start to the New Year. Though, with his luck, he wouldn't hold his breath that it would continue.

CHAPTER TWO

AVERY TOOK A long draught of coffee. She leaned against the counter, eyes closed, as the warm liquid slid down her throat and into her nervous system. My goodness, she'd needed that. Whoever made the hospital shift-change roster hadn't taken midnight kisses and sleepless nights thinking about sexy cowboys into consideration.

Valentina, the ER charge nurse, sidled up alongside her, slipping her own enormous reusable coffee mug onto the counter Avery was using as a support.

"Late night?" Valentina asked.

Avery laughed and *mmm-hmm'd*. It had been, but not for the reasons Valentina's saucy tone was implying.

Well…

For about thirty deliciously juicy seconds it had been. And after that—after walking away from a man who could get a full-time job as a city power grid—surprise, surprise, she hadn't been able to get to sleep. It was the kind of chance encounter the most heartbreaking love songs were written about. But she didn't sing them anymore, so instead she'd just lain there, brushing her fingers along her lips, wondering what it would've been like to have more. Then stridently reminding herself *over* and *over* that she didn't do relationships anymore. Especially not with guitar-wielding, mechanical bull–riding sex gods. Not that a relationship had been on offer. She couldn't see a guy like that hanging up his hat long enough to gather dust, so...

So long, Carter Booth. May your ride into the sunset be as beautiful as your behind.

She tipped her head toward Valentina's impressive mug. "How many cups can you fit in that thing?"

Valentina gave an indignant little huff and said something in Spanish that sounded a lot like, *Takes one to know one, chiquitita.* "I'm not as young as I used to be, *mija*. I need two cups just to get my eyelids open. Then I pour the rest of the pot straight on in. Any room that's left gets filled up with creamer."

Avery leaned in and sniffed. "Hazelnut?"

Valentina tapped the side of her nose, then turned her attention to the board where staff were gathering for the morning handover from the nightshift crew. The night nurse manager looked burned-out and, because it was still busy, was fastidiously moving from curtained bed to curtained bed. Saint Dolores Hospital—aka St. Dolly's—was full to the brim with people who'd been hoping for a spectacular start to the New Year. They'd got that, all right. Not necessarily the type of spectacular they were hoping for but…they'd have a story to tell and, with any luck, the vim and vigor to tell it.

"Looks like we've got a lot of leftovers from last night," Valentina said, nodding at the full patient board. "New Year's Eve seems to bring out the stupid in people."

Avery quickly scanned the list of injuries. There were, of course, a few of the "bread and butter" cases. Chest pain. Abdominal pain. Foreign objects where they shouldn't be. A "concerning" growth.

She grimaced. She'd try to steer clear of that one.

Because there'd been a lot more alcohol flowing on the streets of Nashville last night and the snow had frozen as fast as it had fallen, a truckload of sprains and breaks and…ha!…a fractured coccyx from riding a mechanical bull. She wondered if… No. A man with a butt as firm as Carter's—yes, she'd watched as he'd walked away and climbed up atop that bull—a butt like that wouldn't bruise. Which meant the man behind that particular curtain wouldn't be Carter. No. That ship had definitely sailed. Shame. She'd never been one for one-night stands, but...there were always exceptions to rules. And if there weren't, there should be in his case. She closed her eyes and could practically feel his lips descend upon hers again.

"What're you thinking about?" Valentina gave her a nudge. "It looks naughty, whatever it is."

Avery smirked. "Nothing. Just thinking that New Year's Eve has a lot to answer for."

Valentina clucked her tongue. "Pray do tell. I've got to live vicariously these days."

Valentina had been married over twenty years and was allegedly enjoying being an empty nester, but as soon as her kids had up and left for college, she'd pretty much adopted Avery. Not that Avery was an orphan, but her own parents had... Well... She refused to judge them after what they'd been through. What they all had. They'd run away from the painful memories and she'd dug in. Around the edges anyway.

Valentina lowered her voice to a whisper as the gathering of staff around them thickened.

"I forgot to ask. Did you get the money? From the bull-thingy?"

Avery grinned. "Sure did." Her brain circled right back to the kiss she'd stolen afterward. She forced her smile to appear more innocent. "I should be able to put the deposit down as soon as I can get to the realtors."

Valentina gave her a side hug. "I'm so proud of you, honey. It took a lot of work to get to this point."

About two hundred overtime shifts, upgrading her nursing degree from oncology nurse to acute care nurse practitioner and pinching her pennies on an apartment that had just about enough room to turn around in. With her lease soon up, she would've moved back home, but her parents had decided traveling around the country in a Winnebago was their new destiny. They'd offered her some money toward the deposit, but the sting of their departure had made her refuse it. She wanted to do this on her own. For April.

Her brain slammed on the brakes as it usually did when she thought of her sister. But then, remembering the milestone she'd reached last night, she forced herself to think the words, *Now that April was gone, things were different.*

And they were. For the four hundred and twenty-seven days and—she glanced up at the wall clock above the patient board—two hours and nineteen minutes since her sister had died.

Her jaw clenched. Thinking about those final moments, April's hand in hers, still felt as raw as it had on the day itself. Like losing an actual physical part of herself.

Being able to put a deposit down on the house the two of them had dreamed of owning was the first time in a long time she'd felt a genuine sense of achievement. Sure, getting her nurse practitioner certificate had been big, but the main reason she'd done it was so that she never had to go back to the cancer ward again. In fairness, the work here in the ER was amazing. So, no regrets on that front.

And since the cancer had proved to be a stronger force than they'd thought, the future she and her sister had dreamed of leading in the house wouldn't happen. April teaching, Avery nursing, the pair of them singing down at The Bluebird Café on Thursday nights, hoping to be discovered.

So, yeah. That was different, too. She'd need a housemate to make the mortgage payments. A loan to pay a builder to help her get the place weatherproofed. And a list about as long as her arm for everything else the place would need, but, even so, she still felt proud. As if she'd reached a proper crossroads moment when she could finally visit April's grave and say, *You know what, big sis? I've done it. Made one of our dreams come true.*

As for the others…

"All right, everyone!" Dr. Leah Chang, the head of the ER Department clapped her hand against her tablet to get their attention. Her ebony hair was broken up by her trademark neon streak. Hot pink today. As usual, the entire slick of hair was pulled into submission by a high-set ponytail. "First things first. Happy New Year. I hope you all had fun but that none of you need Breathalyzers today. Ha-ha." Her smile turned serious. "I'm not kidding. If I have any doubts, you're out on your ear."

Avery and Valentina exchanged a look. It was a risk not worth taking. Pity the fool who showed up in Leah's ER nine sheets to the wind.

Leah continued, "New Year. New staff. First up, we've got Rocky Martinez, joining us as an orderly. He is replacing KC Burns, who has moved to Georgia to be closer to his grandmother. Can we have a round of applause welcoming Rocky, please?"

Avery followed Dr. Chang's finger. Her eyes landed on a Latino man about her height who was swirling a set of car keys on his pinkie finger. He pocketed them when he felt the crowd's eyes on him. He was quite obviously a gym buff. He looked like he'd dragged his car here by his pinkie finger rather than driven it.

After a quick round of clapping, Dr. Chang carried on. "He's won an actual medal in the actual Olympics for boxing, so please do not try to arm wrestle him. You will not win. And now, to my… Where'd he go? There he is, behind Avery… Also joining us today, from the wilds of Texas, is Dr. Carter Booth! Another round of applause please."

Avery was midway through putting her hands together when the name registered.

Every hair on her body stood at attention as little sparks of excitement shot through her. She could've turned around and checked. Apparently, he was that close. But looking Carter Booth in the eye after she'd kissed him the way she had felt like throwing herself into a river she'd never be able to swim out of. His current was too strong. Too intoxicating. Not to mention the fact she'd told him he owed her. Would he try to pay his debt? Just thinking about it swept a fistful of glitter through her erogenous zones.

Well, then. Looks like she knew where her body stood on the issue of payback. The only question was could common sense overrule it? It better had, seeing as they were at work.

Rather than turning around and finding out if it was the same Carter Booth who'd all but imprinted himself on her DNA, she sniffed. Last night, she'd inhaled him like he was her last breath of oxygen. He had smelt that good. Pine needles and beeswax. Maybe something else, too. Pheromones that spoke to her with a loudspeaker. Her body shuddered as the scent poured into her nervous system.

"What?" She heard his voice low and sexy in her ear. "Not good enough for applause?"

His tone wasn't accusatory. More…amused. His baritone was so rich it practically vibrated down her spine, lighting up body parts that shouldn't be sparking right here in the middle of a staff meeting. Or ever.

She tilted her head to the side, popped on a smile, pitter-pattered her hands together and stage-whispered, "Happy?"

"Very."

Damn. She shouldn't've looked. For whatever reason, she hadn't noticed his eyes last night. Maybe it was all the neon lights. The chaos he'd wrought in her brain. Maybe it was the fact she hadn't been able to stop staring at his mouth that, annoyingly, looked just as edible now as it had last night. Especially when he dragged his top teeth across his bottom lip when he said words with Vs in them. Like *very*. And *Avery*.

She forced herself to look back up into those eyes of his. Framed by blacker than black lashes, they were just about the most beautiful shade of green she'd ever seen. And green was her favorite color. He still had that "rough and ready" look he'd worn last night: unshaven, tousle-haired, eyes bruised with a lack of sleep. An aura hung around him—a vital potency— that suggested he'd pile into a fight for honor if need be, his or someone else's, but he'd rather not. It wasn't reluctance. It was more…he was a thinking man. The type who didn't just leap into things willy-nilly, which did make her look at what happened last night in a brand new light. She'd taken him for a chancer, but she saw now that she was wrong. Sure, he still had a sting of danger about him, but standing tall, shoulders back, body filling out his dark blue scrubs the way only a few men could, there was something…capable…about him. Something that suggested he'd hang around. For the duration of his shift anyway. And that scared her. Because ten minutes of his time last night had made a deep enough impression on her. And now a ten-hour shift? She wasn't sure if she had the backbone for that.

Avery felt Valentina's eyes bouncing between

the pair of them. Her stomach clenched. She couldn't ignore her. Neither did she want to answer the question she knew was coming.

"Do you two know each other or something?" Valentina asked. "I'm getting a *vibe*."

Avery said, "No," at exactly the same moment Carter said, "Sure do."

"Oh?" Valentina arced an eyebrow.

Shoot. Valentina really was living vicariously through her colleagues.

"He was one of many in a very large crowd down on Honky Tonk Row last night."

"From the looks of things, he stood out." Valentina didn't even try to wipe the smirk off her face.

Carter looked at Avery expectantly, as if he, too, was curious to know whether or not he'd stood out from the crowd. Idiot. Of course, he had. But he was meant to be riding off into the sunrise right now, not showing up in her ER in her city on the first day of the rest of her life.

"She doesn't look best pleased to see you," said Valentina.

"No," Carter agreed. "She doesn't."

"I am perfectly happy to see him," Avery spat back.

Carter laughed. "In which case, thank you for the warm welcome." He tipped an invisible cowboy hat.

"Whittacker." Dr. Chang was making a bee-line for her. "Can you take Dr. Booth here on the grand tour? Help him through the first couple of patients so he knows where to get things and who to call if he needs help." She didn't pause to find out if Avery was amenable to this request. Which, for the record, she was not. "After that, they need you up on the executive floor to discuss this year's benefit. They know it's a tough one for you. Especially after last year, but…" She held up her hands. "I'll leave it to you to discuss the particulars." She gave them a stern look. "Thirty minutes max for the whistle-stop and first two patients. After that, I want both of you moving on double time." She disappeared in a cloud of barked orders.

Talk about being squished between a rock and a hard place.

"C'mon, then," Avery said, turning her back on Carter and swinging her arm in the direction of the busy ER. "Tour first, then we'll get ourselves to work."

"Want to go up to the executive floor first?"

She glowered at him.

He shrugged as if it meant nothing to him, which, of course, it shouldn't. "You just looked as if you might want a bit of backup."

"I can handle it," she said with a bit too much flair.

No, she couldn't. Singing in a benefit for the cancer ward in a concert she usually sang with her sister? Not. A. Chance.

He locked her into one of those impenetrable gazes of his. "I'm sure you can handle whatever you set your mind to, Avery Whittacker."

He took his time saying her name. Deliberately. And, as if he knew it was a lure, he dragged his teeth over his lower lip again. Her breasts gained about ten pounds in that nanosecond. Jerk. He wasn't playing fair.

"We'd better get a move on, Dr. Carter. Dr. Chang likes patients admitted within thirty minutes of arrival and discharged or reallocated to another department within the same amount of time."

He let out a low whistle that ribboned around her chest. "Guess we'd better maximize our time together, then."

She race-walked him through the area as if they were being timed. Ambulance entrances, walk-in registration, trauma, resus, staff lounge, medical storage, critical-care beds, triage and the double doors that led everywhere else: labs, radiology, inpatient wards and, for his purposes, the operating theaters. The moment they hit the supplies cupboard and paused for breath, she knew it was a mistake.

They were alone for the first time and her

parting line to him last night kept rolling through her head—*I guess you owe me, then.*

She was the one who owed him. She'd seen what he'd done. Fallen off when he could've ridden that mechanical bull till the sun rose if he'd wanted to. That's why she'd kissed him. Okay, sure. She thought he was hot as blue blazes as well, but he'd thought of her dignity and he'd preserved it. Let her walk away with a cash prize that could easily have been his.

Now, here, in the close confines of the storage room, her body was her worst enemy. It craved his touch. Same as his wanted hers. She could feel it. Like they were magnets structurally drawn to one another. "So this is where it all happens, is it?" His smile was mischievous. And inviting.

"If you're talking about catheters, enema packs and kidney dishes, yes." She beamed up at him. From a distance. Getting intimate with Carter Booth would be like pulling open a bag of potato chips. Once you got the taste for him, you would always want more.

The sensation of wanting more was something she hadn't felt in a long time. If she were to believe her last boyfriend's parting words to her—*you barely give, and you definitely don't receive*—she wasn't really a strong candidate for a relationship. At the time, he'd been right.

She hadn't been remotely available on the emotional front. Everything she'd had was poured into helping her sister. And physically... Who wanted to make love to someone they knew wasn't really there? She hadn't begrudged the guy for calling it quits. It had meant she'd had more time with April. Three precious months. And, if the rumor mill was anything to go by, her ex was set to head down the aisle this coming Valentine's Day. So, yeah. That ship had sailed. Even so...it wasn't as if she didn't appreciate a bit of eye candy. Looking but not touching was allowed. Right?

Carter pretended to look around. "Where are the personal touches? Fluffy pillows, colored blankets, scrubs with bunny rabbits on them?"

She harrumphed. She didn't know what sort of ERs he'd worked in before, but those sorts of things weren't found in this part of the hospital. Pediatrics? Definitely. Ortho had a blue room for healing vibes. Geriatrics had an orangery and even Imaging had a glassed-in garden room. But here? The part of the hospital where they covered everything from alcohol poisoning to stab wounds and back again? As far as emergency rooms went, theirs definitely wasn't horrible. Not like the ones they showed on TV. But apart from the play area they'd set up in the pediatric waiting area, a handful of potted ficus trees and the quiet zone for people who knew they were waiting for bad news… Nah. Plain scrubs, white pillowcases and ready-wash blankets were where they peaked. "People who come to the ER are in and out, one way or another, before they can admire the soft furnishings. Perhaps you'd be best finding another department if that's your idea of patient care."

He stopped whatever it was he was going to say and looked at her. Really looked at her. "I'd bet every penny I own that you care. Some might say too much."

In that moment, she felt more seen than she had in her entire life. Straight through to her soul.

She did care too much. It was why, after April had lost her life in the very ward she'd dedicated herself to for six years, she simply couldn't do it anymore. Not nursing in general. That was an intrinsic part of who she was. But the oncology ward… Yeah, she wasn't stepping foot in there ever again.

Not all cancer patients were long-termers, but a lot of them were. And, despite her best efforts, she'd got to know them and love them like they were family by the time the inevitable happened. When April had arrived for her first treatment for stage two esophageal cancer, it had just about killed Avery. Not only had life been cruel by giving April cancer, it had taken away that beautiful voice of hers. The one thing April cherished. Being able to sing. If Avery could've done the chemo and the radiation therapy and lost her hair for her, she would have. Donated every pint of blood in her body if it had been a match. Died for her. But life didn't work like that. It was cruel and, sometimes, completely indifferent. Each day that stretched out after April's death seemed to be proof of it…until now. With this man. In this supply cupboard. Who was looking straight into her heart and not running for the hills.

Carter shifted his weight from one hip to the other. "Does it suit you? The drive-through medical care?"

The comment hit its mark. Her conscience. "You like pushing buttons you have no business pushing, don't you?" And then she got angry. "And don't you even dare suggest I give my patients anything other than my best."

She swished out of the room past him and flicked out the light. "We've got patients to see. Chop-chop, Dr. Booth. Time's a wastin'."

CHAPTER THREE

CARTER WOULD'VE HAPPILY walked behind Avery Whittacker for the rest of his life if it would afford him this view—a pert behind that swished beneath the worn cotton of her green scrubs. Shoulders and arms swinging this way and that as if they were about to launch themselves into a dance move. But he couldn't shake the feeling that he'd rattled her cage too hard. Normally, he wouldn't care. Normally, he wasn't in town long enough *to* care. But this time— apart from the fact he might be in Nashville upward of a year—he was getting the feeling he had met Avery for a reason. That the universe had put them together. For him to teach her something or maybe it was the other way around. Maybe both.

Whatever it was, this midnight cowgirl had crawled under his skin and stayed there. The New Year's kiss had a lot to do with that. He hadn't been intimate with a woman in some time and if he'd been the sort to dream of a kiss, it was exactly the type he would've conjured up. Hot, hungry and keen to satisfy.

He shelved the thoughts, knowing they'd only make wearing form-fitting scrubs awkward.

After a brisk walk, they arrived back in the heart of the internal observation zone. An area, he was informed, where they were to keep patients vertical in easily cleaned recliners rather than beds, because once they were lying horizontal in a bed, it meant more specialized staff would be required, and on New Year's Day they were in short supply.

Fair enough. He'd worked in hospitals more bare-boned than this one.

Avery pulled back a curtain to reveal an elderly gentleman who had his hands folded over his heart. He wasn't hooked up to anything, so most likely not a heart attack. His cheeks were more pinked up than your average senior citizen, but his pallor wasn't great. Nor was there a concerned relative sitting by his side. The poor man was either a victim of so-called granny dumping—abandonment by a family who didn't want to look after him—or on his own. Neither of which were good enough in his opinion.

He glanced at the tablet Avery was holding

out for him. High temperature. Tight cough. Rapid, shallow breathing. He popped on a smile. "Mr. Blackstone. What brings you to St. Dolly's this fine morning? Something about a cough that won't loosen up?"

Mr. Blackstone looked as if he might be in disagreement with Carter about how nice the morning was, but he could see he'd disarmed the gentleman with his smile and, after giving the man's liver-spotted hand a gentle shake, his touch, as well. It always killed him to let go when he felt the hands hold on a bit longer than necessary. Warming the head of his stethoscope, Carter got down to business. "That's right, if you could just lean forward for me. Let my hand take the weight of your chest and hang on while I get a good listen." Mr. Blackstone, as he suspected, began to cough as Carter took his weight in his hand.

He pressed the stethoscope to his back, aware of Avery's eyes on him as he heard what he'd suspected. Hints of pneumonia.

He pulled a wheeled stool over so he was at eye level with the gentleman. No one liked being talked down to. Literally or figuratively. "Has anyone run you through the greetings questionnaire?"

Both Avery and Mr. Blackstone gave him a questioning look.

"It's a quick little 'How Are You, Really' quiz I like to give all of my patients."

Mr. Blackstone frowned at Carter as many of them did but nodded to go ahead. He took the man's hand in his and pressed his fingers to his pulse point. Weak, but steady.

"How are you?"

"Been better. I was hoping you might be able to change that."

"That's the plan." Good. He was honest and compos mentis enough to know what was going on. If it was what he suspected, it wasn't too late to dial back the symptoms. "Who brought you here today?"

"My niece."

Something loosened in his chest. Okay. So he had family.

"She coming to pick you up?"

He nodded. "She was finding a parking spot. Said it was too far for me to walk."

That tight knot in his chest grew looser still. "That's nice to hear. So have you had this cough for a while?"

"No." Mr. Blackstone shook his head. "I had a touch of a cold, but then I thought I'd show the whippersnappers how we used to celebrate New Year's and things got a bit out of hand."

Carter and Avery exchanged a look. "How's that, exactly?"

"Well, we went ice-skating out on the pond behind the house and one thing led to another and when I was showing off my double Axel, I fell in."

"What? Into the pond?"

"Yessir. First time in sixty years, and I'm not a little annoyed with myself."

It was the first glint of humor they'd seen in him and any other concerns Carter might've had were now laid to rest. He was a well-looked-after, lively gentleman who could ice-skate well enough to hoick himself into the air and crash through the ice. Perhaps not an ideal situation, but solvable. He rattled through protocol to stave off pneumonia and, when the niece appeared, desperately worried and with a small child on her hip, he gave them a list of symptoms to look out for which would require a return.

"I don't like hospitals," said Mr. Blackstone. "Never have."

"I am very much in agreement, sir," said Carter. "Best thing you can do is submit to any coddling this young woman here is going to subject you to, otherwise you will end up in a bed here on an oxygen tank."

Mr. Blackstone looked at him in horror. The niece practically glowed with gratitude. And if he weren't mistaken, he'd just earned himself a fractional nod of respect from Avery. Job. Done.

* * *

The next patient, a thirty-two-year-old called Mr. Earl Boston, wasn't nearly as obliging. Nor, Carter supposed, would he be if he'd dislocated his shoulder in the process of clambering out of a dumpster after suffering multiple lacerations at the hand—or paw, really—of a raccoon who, it turned out, did not want his help getting out of said dumpster. The cuts were bad. They needed to be flushed. And if his shoulder injury was left untreated, the blood supply to a few critical veins and nerves would be cut off. Mr. Boston also stank to high heaven and had the unsettled disposition of a man who wanted a pain prescription. And not just for the pain. Which made things tricky.

"Have you seen one of these before?" Carter asked Avery.

"I have not." They both tried to keep their expressions neutral. He could tell Avery had also noted what he'd seen in the patient's temperament, because it had taken some assistance from Rocky to get the gentleman from the ambulance bay where the paramedics had clearly had enough.

Mr. Boston was most likely an opioid addict who'd gone dumpster diving only to discover someone—or in this case something—else had got there first. Though dislocated shoulders were common enough, normally they were posterior or anterior dislocations, usually from sporting activities or, in the case of someone like Mr. Blackstone, a fall. But this…this was an inferior dislocation, and it was difficult to keep a straight face, seeing as the guy looked like he was permanently raising his hand to ask a question.

"Stop smirking," Avery growled into his ear.

He had half a mind not to, just to keep her this close, but even a blind man could see she was growing impatient being on babysitting duties with him. She was a nurse practitioner. Could've easily treated the patients they'd seen on her own. But he liked having her near him.

"Sir, if you could please take a seat?" Avery was gesturing to the recliner. "The doctor needs to relocate your shoulder."

"Why don't you do it?" Carter suggested to Avery.

She looked at him in surprise. "Don't you want to?" she asked.

"Not if you haven't done it. This is a teaching hospital, isn't it?"

"Yes."

"Huh," he said when she didn't volunteer anything beyond that. "Guess you're not interested in learning."

"I am so."

"Well, then." He kept his satisfied smile to himself and nodded at her to take up pole position. "Okay, now. Mr. Boston? This might hurt a little, but not as much as it will keeping your arm up like that for the rest of your life."

Earl scowled at him. "Aren't you going to give me anything for the pain?"

"Nope."

The scowl deepened.

Carter took a step forward. "I'll sit on you if you like, to keep you still, but I'm guessing you'll be able to stay nice and still on your own while Nurse Whittacker here does her job."

Earl did a double take. "What? She's not a doctor."

Avery glowered at Carter. It was a look he knew well. One that said, *Wouldn't it be easier if you did this yourself?*

She was right. It would. But then she wouldn't get the practice and he wouldn't be able to tell how high this guy was or wasn't.

He ignored the look and after informing the patient that he was going to be treated by a highly qualified nurse practitioner who knew how to do just about everything short of heart surgery, he began talking Avery through what to feel for and how to perform the reduction. "That's right." He guided her hand along the shoulder, highly aware of the stiffening of her spine. "So, the top of the humeral head is displaced downward rather than toward the back of the body like a posterior one. It's stuck here, under the glenoid rib. Can you feel the difference?"

She nodded, then checked Mr. Boston's other shoulder. They had to cut his shirt off, which created a bit of a hullabaloo that was quickly settled when Avery informed him they'd get him something warmer and cleaner from the lost and found. She returned to his right arm and took ahold of it at the elbow with one hand. Carter stopped her. "You're a leftie, aren't you?"

She nodded, her eyes narrowing briefly as she took on the fact that he'd noticed something a lot of people didn't. He raised his own left hand. "Takes one to know one. If it were me, I'd reposition myself a bit like this."

She flinched just enough to let him know he was too close for comfort. Completely fair enough. This was work and flirting was something that didn't belong here. Especially if it was digging as deep into her psyche as it was in his. Best to keep things professional.

He struck a pose a good arm's length from her, keeping an eye on Mr. Boston as he did, then guided her through the steps. He watched carefully as she eased the humeral head back up and over into the glenoid fossa. Gave a little fist pump when the telltale clunking sound elicited a yowl from Mr. Boston and an ear-to-ear grin from Avery. She'd done the procedure as fluidly as if she'd done it a thousand times.

"Well, that was a new one for me," she said once they'd flushed out the patient's lacerations and put topical antibiotics and numbing agents on the wounds that required stitches, a treatment which, once again, Carter had overseen rather than performed, enjoying seeing Avery at work. Not for a power trip. It was more... He already knew he could have treated the guy with his eyes closed. Rather it was nice to see another medical professional who clearly took pride in her work and cared about the way she treated the patient, no matter how cantankerous they were or how chaotic things were on the other side of the curtain, which, unsurprisingly for New Year's Day, was the case. Once Mr. Boston had been discharged and they were finishing up the paperwork, she nodded toward the exit. "I saw that you gave him the forms for rehab."

Carter nodded. He had. The poor guy ticked pretty much every box that would make him eligible for a medically monitored detox. No job, no savings, no health insurance and a ranking that no one would fight him for on the poverty scale.

"Think it'll do anything?"

Carter shrugged. "You know what they say about horses."

She smiled. "What? That you can lead them to water…"

"…but that you can't make them drink?" They shared a smile of understanding. The heat of it hit him right in the solar plexus. He wanted more from this woman. More than a mutual love of treating patients to the best of their ability. He didn't deserve it, but he wanted it anyway. "Where'd you learn to ride like that?"

She blinked in a deliberate way that made him think she liked to keep her personal life just that. "My grandparents," she said. "My Pawpaw, really. He used to ride the circuits."

Carter grinned. "Rodeo boy? Was he a bull rider or an all-rounder?"

"All-rounder, but he was a softie, really. Didn't like seeing any of the animals getting hurt, so he only barrel raced toward the end of his career. Did some bareback. Mostly, he took on horses other people couldn't train."

Something flashed through her eyes he couldn't nail down. Something fiercely loyal and edged with pain.

"But he still taught you to hang onto a bull?"

Her jaw tightened, then released. "He taught me a lot of things."

Carter suddenly understood what she was saying. He held his hands to his chest. "I'm guessing he's not with us anymore?"

"No, sir," she said briskly and then, as if a flick had been switched, popped on a smile he'd seen her use earlier with Mr. Boston. The kind that said they were done now. "I think you know your way around well enough now, Dr. Booth. You through needing your hand held?"

He couldn't help himself. "I'll sure miss your caring touch."

He was gratified to see the glint of attraction flare up again, even if only fleetingly. "I'm pretty sure you'll be able to hold your own." She handed him the tablet they'd been using and pointed him toward the board. "On you go. You're a big boy now. No more need for training wheels."

He walked away. Slowly. Normally he would've strode, got on with business, but something told him she'd be staring at his butt right now. She'd been doing it all morning. Was probably itching to give it a squeeze, too, but that was just a guess, or maybe a wish, because he knew his own fingers were struggling to mind their own business when it came to close proximity with Avery Whittacker. They would. He respected boundaries, and a woman's boundaries in particular, but he wouldn't be sad if she let down her guard and invited him back into that supplies room.

He examined the board and felt his jaw tighten as his eyes landed on his next patient. A young man with sickle cell anemia.

Just like his sister. But different, of course. This kid was battling puberty as well as the frequently fatal disease. It had taken Carter's father without too much fight. His sister… She fought it, all right. She fought absolutely everything. Their parents when they'd been alive. The law. Him. Incarceration. Doctors. Lawyers. Anyone who tried to set down some rules. Like, *How 'bout keeping yourself alive, for starters?*

He pulled back the curtain and gave the kid a big old grin. He was African American, which wasn't unusual, the majority of US sickle cell sufferers were. His Caucasian sister and father's diagnoses were comparatively rare.

Poor kid looked wiped out. No surprise given he was in the throes of a pain episode. Those misshapen sickle cells the ones meant to be carrying oxygen around his body —had got stuck somewhere in one his smaller blood vessels and clogged the blood flow.

"So… Reece Derby… What brings you to my fine ER today?"

"Fainted."

"Just…fainted?" Carter didn't rise to the attitude the kid was throwing at him. His sister had been like this and a thousand times worse, so…better out than in, son.

"Have you taken anything? For the pain?"

Reece shook his head.

His mother sighed. "Reece, I put some ibuprofen in your backpack for exactly this reason! You don't want to have to take the morphine again. Not with your crazy schedule." She sent an appealing look at Carter. "I bet you he wasn't drinking enough water. He never does when he's out playing with the boys."

Teenaged boys weren't really known for paying much attention to their mother's warnings. And sick ones… Well. He knew all about that. Then again, a *crazy schedule* probably wasn't the best thing for a kid prone to overdoing it and, if things went wrong—which they could, and quickly—a candidate for pneumonia, acute chest syndrome, spleen infections and any number of other things.

"Rightio, Reece. I'll just check out your heart rate and a couple of other things if you don't mind."

Reece sat up with a huff and pulled off his shirt. He was tired and cranky, and from the way he kept slumping back, he was ticking off all indicators of anemia. If it was bad, he might need a blood transfusion. If not…a good steak might help kick his iron count back up.

"You having trouble breathing?"

"No, sir."

"Let's see those eyes of yours."

Reece tipped his head back. They weren't jaundiced, but they weren't exactly bright and bursting with life.

The kid didn't look like a tearaway. Not in the way his sister was. Apart from the super trendy sneakers and the latest release phone, he almost looked like a nerd. Christmas presents, no doubt. Or, as they'd been known in his house, contrition. His dad knew buying his sister a new dress or new shoes wouldn't take away the disease he'd passed on, but it was the only way he knew how to say he was sorry.

They ran through a few more tests and, as a precaution, Carter suggested they head on upstairs to his regular doctor in the Hematology Department. They exchanged fist bumps and extracted a promise from his mom to make steak with plenty of salad on the side tonight. When the kid's mother went to fill out a couple of forms, Carter fixed the boy with a stern look. "You know this can kill you, right? If you don't listen to your body?"

"Yes, sir." The poor kid hung his head and shook it. He knew all right. He looked up at

Carter. The pain he was feeling inside had worked its way through to his eyes. "I just want to be normal, you know? Be like the other kids."

"I know. And for the most part, you can be. Just…let your mom know you hear her and she'll back off a bit. She just loves you is all and that's no bad thing."

Reece smiled at him and once again they bumped fists. He went and joined his mom, throwing a gangly arm around her shoulders, saying he'd be happy to make dinner if she was tired. The moment hit him in the gut like a well-aimed boot.

Why the hell Cassidy couldn't have been more like that was beyond him. Choosing a life of hanging out with actual friends sounded much more fun than finding a crowd who got her locked up for one to three years, behavior dependent.

She'd never wanted to be *normal* he reminded himself, tapping out the notes on Reece's chart. She wanted to be superhuman. If only there'd been some way to pull all of those deformed cells from her body and put them in his own…

He let the thought wither and die. No matter how much he wished for it, he'd never be able to extract the disease from her body and put it into his. Give himself the curtailed life expectancy. Let her live a normal life. There had been days when he'd cursed his parents for taking the risk of having another child after he had been born free of the inherited disease. But despite her problems, the world would be a less interesting place without his little sister, so… warts and all, he loved her.

Maybe the fact he knew where she'd be for the foreseeable future would change things. Maybe it wouldn't. When he'd gone into med school—a place he'd told her he had to stay in if she wanted her rent paid, clothes to wear, food to eat, that sort of thing now that their parents had passed—she'd settled down for a bit. But the week he'd officially become a doctor, she'd bolted. Stolen some candy or some such, and not for the sugar high. Ended up in juvenile detention. And so the cycle continued. When he was being extra honest with himself, he knew the chances of her walking around free, with an ankle bracelet, or on probation, anytime soon was neither here nor there. Until she stopped seeing her disease as something that put her above the law, it plain old didn't matter.

He caught a glimpse of Avery disappearing behind a curtain with an elderly woman using a walking frame. He liked the way she gave the patient space, but made it clear she was close to hand to help no matter what. He shifted his stance. Who was he kidding? He liked near enough everything he knew about Avery Whittacker. It was a short list, but he knew enough of what mattered. She was a good person. She honored family. She was full of grit. And she cared. About her friends, her patients and, for about thirty very sweet seconds, she'd cared about him.

He'd have to nip whatever was happening between the two of them in the bud. If Cassidy's track record for getting herself transferred to yet another so-called correctional facility—he'd yet to see any correcting—was anything to go by, he'd have to leave again soon. He already had a feeling his heart would be the one that broke if he let himself develop feelings for Avery. He'd made that mistake once before in med school and the fall out hadn't been pretty. That was the way the cookie crumbled when you were a Booth. But how he wished things were different.

CHAPTER FOUR

AVERY DELETED THE "Take your time thinking about it." text from management and switched her phone screen to the realtor's page. She growled when she saw that, for the fifth day running, she'd missed the opening hours. Her shifts had been chaotic and bled well into overtime. No surprise there. They were always short-staffed this time of year with everyone wanting to spend some hard-earned vacation time with their families.

No family to go home to meant she had little to no excuse to ask for time off herself. Not that she begrudged her work. It was more that the change in routine was still new enough—raw enough—to make the loneliness she rarely acknowledged feel fathomless. As families bundled in and out of the ER, she acutely missed being with her own. Hungered for her mom's care packages of leftover Christmas food that she and April used to complain about. *How many turkey sandwiches could a girl eat?* they'd used to complain. What she wouldn't give to have one now.

But, she curtly reminded herself, life was different now and if the experts were to believed, sometimes change could be good.

She still had her weekly video calls from her parents, and to be fair they had invited her out to Arizona to celebrate with them, but…they hadn't exactly begged her to join them. She got it. Being all together again was the most painful reminder that they weren't *all* together again.

She tried not to take it personally. The day they'd adopted her—a scrawny, belligerent mixed race two-year-old with a wild look in her eye—her life had been changed for the better. They'd fed her, clothed her, gave her rules and the room to knee and elbow them into the shape she needed. They'd loved her as if she had been their own. Same as her new grandparents who'd cradled her in their arms, told her bedtime stories and put her on top of her first pony. And, most amazingly, she'd gained a big sister. Her hero from the second they'd laid eyes on one another.

April was the reason behind the adoption. She'd been desperate for a little sister and, despite a few years of trying, her parents hadn't been able to give her one the regular way, so they'd opened up their hearts and brought Avery into their family. So she owed everything to April. The world's best big sister. Voice like an angel. Knew her way around a guitar the way Avery had learned her way around a horse. Dreams big enough for the two of them. Dreams that were meant to have propelled them into the limelight of the Grand Ole Opry. Right up until cancer announced itself in the form of a hoarse voice April couldn't shake, followed by difficulty swallowing, and then a peculiar lump near her collarbone.

When she'd received the diagnosis, Avery had taken to looking after her sister as if it were the sole reason she'd been put on this earth. It had been no surprise when her boyfriend of just over a year had ended their relationship. Told her she wasn't *emotionally available* anymore. To him, she wasn't. To her family, she was all in. She'd moved into her grandparents', helping out with the horses, doing her shifts at St. Dolly's. But mostly she had devoted herself to looking after April.

When April's voice and then her life had been snatched away from her...so had their shared dream of singing professionally one day. Which was why Avery hadn't sung since. Not a solitary note. And why the hospital management wasn't particularly thrilled with her now that it was just a handful of weeks away from the annual benefit that raised money for the oncology ward.

Well, tough. This was Nashville. You couldn't swing a cat without hitting a dozen singers. She got it. There weren't many who'd had sisters die of cancer under their care here at St. Dolly's, but still.

The truth was she was afraid to sing again. Afraid to feel everything that would rise up from that private place only singing tapped into. The place where she held her grief. Her sorrow. Her loss.

It was bad enough that she'd lost her sister and that her adoptive parents hadn't found her reason enough to hang around. But she'd lost her grandparents shortly after April's death, as well. As if life thought she had had too much good luck through the years. Sure. It had given her a bumpy start at the beginning—teenaged birth parents unequipped to raise a child—but from there on out she'd enjoyed the smoothest of sailing for years, only to have it all yanked away over these last eighteen months.

The house she and April had wanted to buy was the one thing that remained. And she'd focused her energies on saving to buy it as if her life depended on it. Praying every night that someone else wouldn't see what she saw in the place. It was a fixer-upper. The kind that was more labor of love than a few rounds with the handyman. And now, at long last, she had the money. For the deposit anyway.

So the fact that Avery still hadn't managed to get down to the realty office to put down the deposit was par for the course. That, or the heavens were trying to send her a subtle hint that she shouldn't buy it. She wasn't so good at reading the signs these days.

"Most health professionals look happy when the patient board is empty."

She didn't turn when Carter slid his forearms onto the same counter she was leaning on, but it was impossible not to respond to his presence. Her body was in total lust with him. Had been for the past week. Handfuls of glitter lit up her insides each time they passed. Butterflies took flight whenever she heard his voice. Her intimate zones had a parade if their hands so much as brushed. Which they may have done. Multiple times.

Even so. Looking him in the eye was another thing altogether. She couldn't shake the feeling that he could read her like a book, and frankly she didn't want to be read. Not today anyway. She was tired and confused and was supposed to be pouring what little energy she had left into making her dead sister's dreams come true. One of them at least.

Carter shifted position to let one of the nurses pass, and as he readjusted that sexy body of his along the countertop, a waft of pine and honeycomb released another fistful of hot sparks in her belly.

An involuntary hum filled her throat, but she caught it just in time, turning it into a throat clearing.

Something about Carter Booth made her want to open up her throat and commune with the songbirds. And it scared her. As if rediscovering that part of herself would be the cruelest of reminders that no matter how hard she'd tried to save her sister's life, she'd failed.

Oh, she knew she alone couldn't cure cancer and that, in the end, no matter how great a nurse she'd been, there was literally nothing she could've done beyond making sure her sister didn't feel any pain.

But it didn't mean she was going to sing again. It would be too savage not to hear her sister's voice wrap around hers like ivy as it always had done. Would it hurt as much as radiation therapy? As much as chemo? As much as dying?

Carter nudged her with his elbow. "You look tired."

"And you look like you could do with a session at the Charm Academy."

Carter snorted.

Avery harrumphed. She wasn't going to admit that he was right. She *was* tired. And hungry. And soon to be homeless as she'd given notice on her tiny apartment rental. She gave Carter a quick glance. He was still looking at her, a smile playing on those stupidly sexy lips of his.

"I don't suppose you can recommend any good places for some Texas barbecue around here?" he asked.

She gave one very slow, very studied blink. "Did you just blaspheme in front of me?"

The corners of his mouth twitched. "What?" He kicked his Texan accent up a notch. "Is mentioning the finest barbecue in the land some form of cussing around these parts?"

"You're damn straight it is! Your piddly little Texas barbecue doesn't hold a candle to our Tennessee slow-cooked pork ribs. Brisket so tender it defies the laws of….um…soft things." She flicked her fingers at him. "Texas Schmexas."

He let out a whoop and clapped his hands together. "That's fighting talk, missy. You do know that barbecue is about as close as you can get to religion where I'm from, don't you?"

"And where is that exactly?" she asked, feeling the vinegar from the sauce she was mentally tasting kicking her energy levels back up to par. "Where you come from."

He eyed her for a minute as if deciding whether or not she was worthy of the information. She jutted out her chin. Damn straight she was.

"I worked at Partridge Hill in Austin."

Wow. They didn't let just anyone walk through those doors and treat patients. It was a good hospital. A renowned one even. "And left why?"

His green eyes darkened, and if she wasn't mistaken, the tiniest of twitches set loose in his jaw. "Family reasons."

She dialed back her aggression. She got that. She also got not wanting to talk about it. The only person allowed to mention her sister was Lia and even then...

Suffice it to say, the two of them were besties because they knew what topics were allowed during their weekly Guac and Talk meets at Gantry's Margarita Den. So even though Carter hadn't explained his family reasons, the way he hadn't moved a muscle but looked as if his entire physique had changed spoke to her louder than the kiss they'd shared, and that thing had announced itself with a bullhorn.

"Guess I'd better learn you up about the finer things in Tennessee, then," she said.

Carter had never been one to put on the plastic bibs most barbecue joints supplied these days but to try to get some sort of reaction from Avery, he tied one on. "What do you think?"

"Cute," she said, her dark eyes dropping back down to the menu.

He grinned. He'd take that as a win. She hadn't smiled or looked all that impressed, but she was sitting across a table from him. Neither of them were talking about it, but that electricity they'd both been ignoring at work was still buzzing loud and clear out here in the real world. Or maybe they'd been drawn together the same way his sister was drawn to trouble. Moths to a flame. The thought sobered him.

He stared at the menu, then feeling shot through with too much choice, set it down again. "What would you recommend, Avery, seeing as you're the expert on regional cuisine?"

She put her menu aside. "I'm guessing that depends upon how hungry you are and how much time you've got."

"Lots and very."

She smiled. "You're a proper wordsmith, aren't you?"

"You want pretty?" He leaned in close enough to smell her—loving the way she somehow wore the scent of sunshine and meadow grass even though it was the dead of winter. "I've never seen a woman ride a bucking bronco—live or mechanical—the way I saw you ride. And to me, that was poetry in motion. Better than grooming a horse. Sending a patient home to heal after a perfect surgery. Or playing lip-lock with a stranger."

She bridled. "Watching me ride was better than kissing me?"

He shrugged. "I suppose they were about equal."

She snorted, then tipped her head to the door. "If that's how you feel, then how about you get your food to go?"

If he'd blinked, he would've missed it, but somehow, he'd caught another glimpse of what he'd convinced himself he'd imagined. A raw vulnerability caught behind walls that instinctively flew up around that tender heart of hers. And something new. Hurt.

He'd pushed too hard. Pushed when he should've pulled. Just like he'd done to a dozen women before her, only those times he hadn't felt the ramifications of his actions in the form of remorse. Well. Once he had and he'd taken it as a lesson well learned. Clearly not that well learned.

Idiot.

"No, ma'am," he said resolutely. "There is no chance I would leave a woman sitting on her own. And definitely not one who's made the type of impression you have."

"And what is that exactly?"

He shook his head, unable, or maybe unwilling, to put into words the fact that she was the first woman to put a chink in his armor since he'd decided relationships weren't for him.

He wasn't a stranger to them. There'd been a girl in high school. Then his dad had died of sickle cell. A couple of long-term flings in college. Then his mother had passed from a stress-induced embolism. Heartbreak if you were to take his sister's word for it. He'd had a long-term relationship in med school. Got too comfortable with things finally going according to plan. Finishing his internship put short shrift to that.

Having a poorly sister hell-bent on getting herself the electric chair instead of dying at the hand of her disease had a way of limiting his options.

Okay. Maybe Cassidy wasn't that bad. A bit of shoplifting here. Some grand theft larceny there. The latest: a DUI after a dine and dash.

She never wanted the stuff. She wanted the high. Well, she'd got that all right. And a three-year sentence that she would definitely be serving at least a year of.

And no, he knew he didn't have to traipse along in his sister's wake, but there was no other family around to keep an eye on her, and prison hospitals weren't exactly elite hubs of medical excellence, so he did. Chasing her around the country, making sure he worked in whatever hospital she'd be sent to if things went south. All of which meant over the years on a personal front, his specialty was being an ass. But right now, he was wishing it were something else.

When he failed to answer, Avery shook her head, irritated, and put down the menu. "I don't have time for game playing, Carter."

"And I don't have a single friend in Nashville." Or anywhere for that matter. Getting close only led to saying goodbye and goodbyes hurt. He let out a silent string of cuss words, then decided, for once, to choose honesty as the best policy. He put his hand on his heart. "I could do with a friend right now. One who kisses like you do would be the icing on the cake. Or the Mississippi mud pie they've got here on the dessert menu if that's your preference."

She gave him the side eye, but something told him she was still sitting here because she was interested. "That sounds like a little bit more than your average friendship would offer."

He feigned innocence. "Mud pie?"

After shooting him a look he couldn't read, he saw her lips fighting a losing battle with her frown and eventually twisting through into a smile. "Sounds risky. And high calorie."

He was about to suggest something that could burn off the calories real quick but thought better of it. Avery didn't strike him as the "dine and dash" type in the romance department.

He waved his menu between them. "Why don't we start with the healthy stuff? And then, if we're still hungry, we can see how we go."

He wasn't talking about mud pie anymore and they both knew it.

Avery seemed to consider the doorway for a second and then, when her stomach gave a loud growl, conceded that it was a good idea. They ordered far too much and as such were told it'd be a bit of a wait. When staring at the smattering of people around them grew awkward instead of interesting, Carter asked, "What part of town do you live in? I'm in a serviced apartment right now and it's just about sucked my soul dry."

She arced an eyebrow. "They're that bad?"

He nodded. "I like somewhere with a bit of heart. Character. These are just cookie-cutter apartments that, whilst convenient, aren't exactly welcoming."

"What kind of houses have you lived in before? Did you have a favorite?"

Carter looked away and then drew his thumbs along his forehead as if trying to make room in his brain for the question. If only there were a simple answer. This kind. This house. This town. The end. "I tend not to hang around long enough anywhere to get a mortgage."

She frowned, then shrugged. "Thought so."

He grinned. "Oh, you did, did you? Already got me pegged for a love 'em and leave 'em kind of guy?"

Where the hell had that come from?

She stared at him as if trying to figure out how best to let him know he wasn't her type. "I just got the feeling you moved a lot, but I wouldn't've said it was because you were leaving a trail of broken hearts in your wake."

Despite himself, he laughed. "You're right. It's a bit more complicated than that."

Most people left the conversation there, but not Avery. "Why? Why is it complicated?"

"My sister. She's a bit... Let's just say her health's not the best and she's got a fairly elastic interpretation of the law."

"So you…what? Is she a minor? Are you her minder?"

"No, she's a grown woman, just behaves like a child. As for the minder bit…" He tipped his head back and forth. "Self-appointed. I'm sure she'd rather I did other things with my time."

"Like buy a house?"

It was a pointed question and one he really didn't know the answer to. For the first time in his life, he hoped so. "I don't know. I'm not sure how long I'll be here."

"Why?"

He debated telling her and then thought, *Screw it.* "My sister's in the state pen."

Her eyes widened but she passed no judgment.

"She's got sickle cell anemia. That and a passion for brushing up against the law."

Avery pushed her lips forward. "Sounds like a tricky combination."

"It is if you're her big brother. And her only living relative."

He saw something change in Avery right then. A shift in her body language that altered the protective energy she'd been holding close to her like a shield. "And that's why you left Austin?"

"And Dallas and St. Louis and New Orleans and—"

She laughed and held up her hands. "I'm guessing that truck of yours has a pretty high mileage count."

He nodded. "Wouldn't get more than five bucks for it if I drove it into a car lot."

The light in her eyes dimmed. "I'm guessing she behaves that way because she figures she's going to die anyway, so why not go down in flames?"

"Damn, girl. You know how to get to the point."

She shrugged as if she had some insight in the matter but offered nothing. *Still waters*, as his mother used to say.

"Look." He put his hands flat on the table. "I'm going to lay my cards out. As you know, I'm new in town and you're pretty much the first and only thing I've taken a shine to. If things go the way they usually do, I won't be here long, but while I am, I sure could do with having a friend."

"What makes you think I want to be your friend?"

A solid fifty-fifty combination of nothing and everything about her. The fact she was still sitting here in this pleather booth spoke volumes. As was the fact she'd yet to take off her coat. The way she blushed whenever he brushed his hand against hers. And turned the other direction to grind her teeth once she had. The way she'd welcomed his tongue into her mouth the other night, letting him explore the heat and hunger he knew they were both feeling all the way down to their toes. The part about how she'd insisted on driving her own car here so she could see herself home after.

"Honestly?" he said. "I think that you like me, but that you don't like that you like me. And that's why I'm proposing a fling without strings."

It was a dare. And she knew it.

"So…you want to sleep with someone who isn't sure if they like you?"

"Quite the opposite. I want someone who knows they like me but isn't interested in anything long-term for all the right reasons."

"And what are those exactly?"

There was only one reason, really. Not getting his heart broken. He took her hands in his and rubbed his thumbs across the backs of them. "Look. Life's too short not to enjoy some pleasure. Especially having met someone who I can tell just by looking at her is a kindred spirit." He gave his heart a thump and was gratified to see her blush. He pressed kisses onto the backs of her hands, then released them. "Look. I'm trying my best to be honest. If we get together while I'm here, I know we can have some fun. And it doesn't have to all be adult time. We can… I don't know… What do you like to do?"

"Dance."

"Good. Excellent. We'll go dancing. Then a few months down the line when I inevitably have to up stakes, nobody's heart gets broken. Easy-peasy."

A fire lit in his belly when he saw in her eyes what he felt in his gut. A hunger for something that was more than skin deep. A fear that going there might destroy her.

The energy between them shifted once again. From sparring to interested. Real interested.

She pushed her menu to the side. "I don't know if I want to have a fling with a traveling Casanova."

He belly-laughed, then crossed his heart. "Trust me. Women can see I resist commitment from a mile off, so I try and dial back the 'man whore' aspect of things." His expression turned serious. "I haven't been with anyone in a while. Short-term or otherwise."

She took a sip of her water, then flicked her dark eyes up to meet his. "We'd keep this between ourselves? The sexy-sexy stuff?"

"If you like." He'd sign a contract in blood if she wanted.

"Okay, then. Friends with benefits." She

lifted her glass to his for a toast, but because he knew better than most that time was a precious commodity, he leaned across the table and kissed her instead.

CHAPTER FIVE

WHEN CARTER BROKE the kiss, Avery's head snapped back as if she'd just been given whiplash. And in a way, she had.

He was calling a spade a spade and asking her to acknowledge it, too.

Okay, sure. Over the past few days, they'd been wriggling along in this direction. Flirty. Not flirty. Spatting. Making the peace. Carter was being adult enough to put into words what they both knew. There was something happening between the two of them and the only way it could be laid to rest was for one of them to leave town or to go for it.

She thought of the holding pattern she'd been in for the past year. The one she'd landed in once she'd emerged from the initial fug of grief after her sister passed. And even before then, her ex had made it pretty clear she wasn't "ideal girlfriend" material. He'd been right. Even all these months later, filling the void her sister left with a relationship did not seem wise. Her heart and mind were elsewhere.

She'd set her sights on buying this house and having it be the answer to all her dreams, but now that she was within a hair's breadth of it... she wasn't sure that a house without April in it would do what she'd been stupidly hoping for. Bring her back.

She looked at Carter. He looked straight back at her. She could tell he wasn't pressuring her. But his offer was serious. "So...when does it start?" she asked. "Our new arrangement."

"Up to you. I'd happily steam up the truck right now, but I don't want you to think I only want you for your body. Believe it or not, I'd like to get to know the real you, as well."

Despite herself, she blushed. It was one thing to lust after someone, another to have him treat her as a whole person—warts and all. It was more than her ex had done. He never would've said as much but she knew deep down that he'd resented her sister's illness because it took away the time and energy she put into their relationship. He'd wanted a 1950s housewife. Not a woman with a career of her own, a dying sister, grief. Good riddance to him.

She looked at Carter.

Could she do this? Enjoy the physical connection she felt with him, but keep her heart safe and secure?

What if this little experiment pulverized what was left of her inner strength?

What if it didn't?

What if it rejuvenated her? Made her feel alive again? Even though she didn't want her ex back, he'd had a point. She'd been walking around like a zombie and it wasn't until she'd laid eyes on Carter Booth that she'd felt the blood pumping through her veins like it used to.

"I don't even know your middle name," she huffed. As if that were a deal breaker.

"Zane," he said. "That help?" His tone was wry but not unkind. He was giving her the space she needed.

The truth of the matter was she liked the idea. Her grandparents had passed. Her parents were gone, broken by the death of their only natural daughter. She was feeling abandoned and trying to fix it by putting a deposit on an empty house that would never know the sound of her sister's voice.

What exactly was she going to do once she moved in there? Sit in the middle of it and cry every day? Maybe having a "friends with benefits" relationship with Carter would make her happy again. Maybe it would only put her grieving on hold.

To their mutual relief, the food arrived and they began to eat. They were hungry enough for the silence to come naturally, but she had no doubt that both of their brains were whirring like a train heading full speed along the tracks.

Could she trust him with her heart? That was the real question she should be asking herself. Even with a plastic bib on, the man exuded an inner power that didn't seem entirely under his control. But that craving for honesty he was talking about, and desire. Suddenly, she wanted nothing more than to pull her nails down both of their facades and see what was underneath.

She finished a pork rib, wiped her hands on a napkin, then deposited it on the growing pile they had on a plate on the side of the table. "I was going to buy a house tomorrow."

His eyebrows went up, the rest of him stayed still. "Oh?"

"Some of that money from the other night is for the deposit." She hesitated for a minute, then plowed ahead. "The plan was to buy it with my sister."

"Ducked out, did she?"

"No." She was shocked to feel the tears that she normally kept at bay sting at the back of her throat. "She died almost two years ago."

Carter's whole body reacted to the information and, unlike most people who felt compelled to instantly offer some meaningless platitude, he gave himself the time to truly absorb what she'd said. Pressing one of his big old hands to his heart, he finally spoke. "I've never found an adequate way to express my condolences. Words don't seem good enough to…well…not with my vocabulary anyway."

"Cancer," she said, surprised to hear herself proactively continuing the conversation. Maybe it was the fact he had a sister in trouble, too. Maybe it was just time. She'd kept the topic locked up so tight she hadn't realized how much it needed air. Maybe if they had this *special friendship*, as he called it, one with no-holds-barred, all of the honesty she hadn't realized she craved, she'd find a way to move forward. It would hurt. She might even let loose all the grief and rage she knew was lurking around her insides like a cornered bobcat.

He was strong. Sure of himself. Obviously liked a challenge. She could give him that. And a whole lot more.

It was on the tip of her tongue to tell him her sister's death was the reason she had left the oncology ward. It wasn't because she hadn't loved the job. She had. Very much. She'd had people reach into her life before she'd been old enough to know how bleak it was. This was her version of paying that generosity of spirit forward. Being there for people during their darkest journeys—it was humbling and hadn't felt like a job so much as a calling. But once she'd been forced to say goodbye to the one person in her life who she'd never imagined saying goodbye to… Well…there were limits to a person's capacity for handling grief.

She'd spent the past eighteen months teetering so close to the precipice of hers… Changing departments and the fact she and Lia had an unspoken agreement *not* to talk about her loss were the only things holding her together. That and earning the money to buy the house.

"Esophageal cancer," she clarified. "It took her voice, her throat and then, finally, all of her."

Carter didn't mince words. "That's a cruel way to go."

"It was." She was pretty sure her face told him everything he needed to know.

He was a doctor so he didn't need the details. And even though St. Dolly's was full to the brim with amazing doctors and nurses, many of whom she considered friends, she felt for the first time since April had died that she was talking to someone who cared. Really cared that she'd loved and lost. Maybe it wasn't even that, because, of course, her friends and family *cared*.

But from the moment they'd laid April to rest, a lifelong fear had resurfaced. The one about being left to fend for herself again. Just as she'd had to when social workers had found her scrabbling around in a dumpster for food when her mother had… Well…her mother had had her own problems. When she'd heard she'd died, the world had carried on as it had before. But when April died… Sea change. So she'd braced herself for the inevitable. And just as she'd feared…the people she held most dear disappeared from her life, one by one, as if she hadn't mattered at all.

So why did Carter Booth, a man who clearly had burdens of his own to shoulder, want to make room for her in his life?

She looked hard into his eyes, trying to catch glimpses of whatever it was he saw when he looked at her. The strength to do the same.

He knew she could ride a bull, boss an emergency room and that her sister had died of cancer.

Not bad for a few days of tactically avoiding one another.

What else?

He knew how she kissed when she wasn't holding back. That she didn't pull punches. And that he unzipped something inside her that made her speak her mind.

"Is that plan still green lit?" he asked after another swig of his beer. "To buy the house?"

"Fifteen minutes ago, I would've said absolutely." She could hardly believe her own ears.

"What changed?"

"You."

His eyebrows dove together. "I wasn't meaning to put a wrench into your plans."

He hadn't. He'd just shone a light on them. "It wasn't you. It was more…" She twirled a couple of French fries around a pool of ketchup. She looked up and met his. "You made me realize I was putting my hopes and dreams into things and you've put yours into people."

He pushed his lips forward, then sucked them back into his mouth. "Person. And let me assure you, doing it my way comes with its own set of problems."

"Sure, but… I don't know why, but you've made me realize that when I buy that house, it isn't going to make my sister come back. It might even make me feel worse."

"Why? Your eyes light up when you talk about it."

"They do?" She felt her cheeks pink up that he'd noticed.

"What do you say you ask for one more tour before you sign on the dotted line? I'll go with you if you want."

She was halfway through saying no when she forced herself to fight the instinct. Shutting people out for the rest of her life wasn't going to bring her sister back, either. He was just another set of eyes on a house he didn't give two hills of beans about. It would be practical to let him come along. "Cool."

"You sure?"

"Yup."

"And…" he swirled a French fry around a puddle of ketchup "…any further thoughts on that other thing?"

She gave him a slow grin. "The 'friends with benefits' thing?"

He nodded.

She felt her temperature spike. Her eyes dropped to his lips.

"You want me, don't you?"

He was grinning as he said it, but she knew if she said no, they'd draw a line under this conversation and never revisit it.

"How far away is your apartment?" he asked.

"You can't swing a cat in mine."

He arced an eyebrow. She blushed. Maybe he thought she was expecting some wild sexual acrobatics. Before she could clarify that she wasn't expecting cartwheels, he said, "Well, then. Looks like you'll be staying with me tonight."

* * *

By the time he managed to get the key in the door, Carter was so hot and bothered he was pretty sure he'd go blind if Avery didn't let him pick her up and carry her to the bedroom. Or the sofa. The floor of the tiny living room would do at this point, but not here in the hall-way. He had his standards.

Plus, there was always the possibility she might suddenly yawn and say, *Not tonight, honey, I've got to wash my hair.* But if he'd been reading the signals right, he was pretty sure the only showers they'd be taking would be together.

Something had uncorked in them while they'd eaten dessert. Sharing that gooey choc-olatey pie had been near enough the sexiest foreplay he'd ever been involved in. Whether it was the sugar rush, the phenylethylamine in the chocolate or good old-fashioned lust, they'd been behaving like a pair of feral teenagers ever since, a lust bubble forming around them as if it protected them from the rest of the world. He hadn't been able to stop touching her. They'd even left his truck at the restaurant because the idea of not being able to put his hands on her shoulders, her cheek, her thighs for the ten-minute drive over to his place seemed a form of torture he didn't have the endurance for. Not tonight anyway.

And judging by the make-out session they'd had in the car before they'd even got in the building... *Mmm...* Suffice it to say, if he'd thought their New Year's kiss had been one in a million, he'd been sorely mistaken. She had dozens more just like it and some that were even better.

"Hurry," she commanded.

Okay. She wasn't going to be washing her hair, then.

"I am. You got me all flustered, woman."

More than that. She'd got him worried. This wasn't going to be a one-night stand. No chance. Nor was it something he could walk away from all free and easy when the time came. He needed to readjust his emotional settings before things went any further.

Avery grabbed the door handle, gave the key a jiggle and twisted it. It swung open. She arced an eyebrow. "You ready now?"

He grinned. Hell, yes. He'd sort any emotional fallout later. Life was for living, right?

She shoved him into the apartment and began unzipping, unbuttoning and unbuckling everything that held him in clothing. All of a sudden, she stopped and held her hands up. "You cool with this?"

"Honey, I am hot and bothered with this." He took ahold of her hips and pressed them to his so that she knew exactly how uncool he was. Her grin was wicked. She pressed into him as if to confirm she liked what she felt, then got back to work. Why the hell he'd worn a shirt with so many damn buttons on it was beyond him. He could just rip the thing off, but feeling her fingers nip and twist against the fabric and his skin wasn't exactly a hardship. He liked seeing this side of her. In the ER, she was all contained, controlled. Hair back. Scrubs immaculate. Face implacable.

Right now? Not so much.

Her hair had long since lost contact with its clips. Her scarf had hit the floor. Coat had quickly followed suit. Her lipstick had vanished and all that remained was raw, unfettered desire. Her charged energy made him feel a lot less apologetic for all of the plans he had in store for that deliciously curvy body of hers.

"I better ask," he said while she'd freed his chest of fabric and swept her hands across the tips of his nipples. "Are *you* cool with it?" He hovered his fingers above the two ribbons barely holding onto the fabric covering her breasts.

She took ahold of the ribbons and tugged them loose. "Icy."

He could barely breathe.

By the time they had scrabbled around for some protection and were skin on skin, Carter could say in full confidence that Avery Whittacker was the polar opposite of icy. She was hot like lava. Steamy like the tropics. A pool of sunlight on a winter's day. Anything and everything he wanted in a woman. Perfection is what she was.

He'd never known a woman like her. And at precisely this moment, she was ravaging his naked body like he was the last man on earth and her only chance of survival. Something he never imagined being for anyone. Their salvation. He caught the emotions that came along with that and sent them packing. Tonight was about Avery and hearing that delicious groan of hers.

The first time around it was exactly as he'd imagined it might be. Hot. Sweaty. Intense. Enough to blow his ability to think straight clean out of the water.

Nice to see reality catching up to his fantasies for once. He wasn't ashamed to admit it. The nights were long and sometimes lonely. So, sure, he'd closed his eyes and pictured being with Avery pretty much every night since they'd met. They'd had their prelude in the car, so from the moment she'd shucked his jeans off him, turned around and slid him inside of her, the lovemaking, such as it had been, had felt more akin to a sexy wrestling match.

Fast. Furious. A bit angry. A bit not. She might've bitten him. He may have scraped his fingers down her back to find out if she'd moan or scream. She moaned. It had been just about the hottest sex he'd ever had. Right up until the second time. They'd both got their wits about them a bit more and, having used up a fair amount of energy in round one, they took their time. He knew he'd need a lifetime to really know her body. The bits of her belly that made her shiver when stroked. The spot on her inner thigh that, when he licked it, made her grab ahold of his hair and demand he never stop. Her lips. They were point-blank the most kissable lips he'd ever had the pleasure of exploring, let alone tasting. She was honeysuckle and hot sauce. Nutmeg and vanilla. Edible is what she was. Head to toe. But he didn't have a lifetime. He had whatever time his sister's sentence, or her health, would give them.

"Hey." Avery held him out at arm's length and looked at him. "What just happened there?"

"Nothing."

"Yes, it did. You pulled back."

Physically, he hadn't, but emotionally he guessed he had. Just like always, he was already counting down to his departure. So much for carpe diem.

He kissed her instead of offering an explanation. And it did nothing to change the way she felt in his arms—right at home. Already, he felt the storm clouds gathering. He could get a little too used to this. Allow those thoughts he'd allowed himself once before—thoughts about putting down roots, getting a house, the picket fence, even the kids. He didn't know why, but he got the feeling Avery was fighting similar demons for different reasons. So as far as feelings went, arm's length was okay by her. He liked that. Having a tacit understanding of one another. An instinct as to when it was right to push, to demand even, and when it was best to let things lie. He pulled her into his arms and matched his breaths to hers. The lines between where his body ended and her body began blurring as sleep eventually began to seep into both of their pores until, with the scent of her surrounding him like a comforting cloud, he fell into a deep dreamless sleep.

A mug of coffee scraping across the bedside table was the first thing he became aware of. A pair of caramel-colored legs wearing a pair of his boxers was next. He scanned up the length of one of his old country music T-shirts, decided it was much nicer with boobs behind it and, eventually, settled on Avery's morning smile. *Mmm...* He reached out, slid a hand up her thigh and tugged her to him.

"Uh-uh, sunshine. We got work. At least I do." She crossed the room and yanked open the curtains. It was still dark. Winter had a lot to answer for. But at least he didn't have to squint.

She flicked on the overhead light.

He rubbed his hand over his eyes, then forced himself to confront the day. His eyes hit the clock and bolted up to standing. "I'm due at St. Dolly's soon. Why didn't you get me up?"

"I don't know your schedule, do I?" she protested, then sniggered. "Besides, you looked cute, all snuggled up there. Like a puppy."

She didn't resist when he pulled her close for a kiss. "Is that what you'd like? A puppy?"

Damn. He shouldn't have gone there. He could already see one bouncing around an imaginary lawn he'd just mowed for her. Taking it to puppy class together. Long walks through the countryside.

She tipped her head side to side as if she were seeing the same pictures and giving the notion some serious consideration. "I can't even get it together to buy a house, let alone the puppy to go in it. I think that's one for the *no* pile, bud. Sorry."

Normally, he would've laughed at how thoughts of puppy ownership pulled them in opposite directions, but it didn't feel funny. It felt sad. Sad and lonely that two people who clearly liked one another the way they did couldn't daydream about the future without producing frowns. Pretty much how his childhood had been, he reminded himself. Why daydream when you knew early death was inevitable?

The memory of his mother's face at his father's funeral twisted his gut into a knot. He didn't wish anyone dead, but he had to admit, he'd almost been relieved for her when an embolism took her shortly after his father. She'd hated life without him, and Carter hated that he couldn't take her pain away. Or his sister's, for that matter. All of which fed into the big pool of evidence that he didn't deserve to dream of puppies or anything else with Avery. Well. Sex. He'd definitely be dreaming about the sex. For a long time to come.

Avery took a gulp of her coffee, clearly not bothered that it was scalding hot, and perched herself on the edge of the dresser.

"Right, my little cowhand. We better set up a few rules and regulations for how we operate at the hospital."

He snorted, then reread her expression. "Oh. You're serious." He took a slug of his coffee, wondering how the hell she didn't flinch drinking something that hot and strong.

She went first. "I don't want anyone to know we have something personal going on."

Fair enough. He wouldn't want to have to leave her to explain everything when he inevitably left, so he was good with that. "Fine."

"If we happen to accidentally meet in a supplies room or an on-call room, we either keep the door fully opened or completely locked."

He suppressed a grin. So they could have hanky-panky at work, just so long as no one knew about it. He would never embarrass her in that way anyhow. Private lives were called private lives for a reason. He put two fingers to his eyebrow and saluted. "Noted."

"And you are never to smile at me like that at work, otherwise my nipples will betray everything."

"What?" Now he was laughing. "Like this?" He tried on a number of smiles.

She wriggled and crossed her hands over her chest, giggling as she screamed, "Stop! It's hard to hide what your nipples are up to when you're wearing scrubs."

"Well, that's something I look forward to seeing." He crossed to her and skidded his thumbs across the soft cotton of her T-shirt just…about… Yup. There they were.

"See?" Avery gave him a warning look. "Nipples are a problem when they are smitten with a hot guy."

"Oh, they're smitten, are they?"

She scrunched her nose and gave a dismissive little sneer. It was cute. Trying to pretend she wouldn't respond if he slipped his hands between her legs and slid his fingers—

She gasped when he carried on sliding his fingers back and forth, back and forth, slow and deliberate as if there weren't a roster full of doctors and nurses waiting for the pair of them. "Carter Zane Booth—"

He stopped her with a hard intense kiss. "Don't you use my full name like I'm in trouble."

"Don't you touch me like that when we're due for work in—" she glanced at the clock "—half an hour."

He didn't stop until she came. When she did, she called out his full name again, but it didn't sound at all like he was in trouble. She pulled him into the shower where they discovered a whole new brand of fast and furious. They dressed, raced to the restaurant to pick up his truck and then made their way to the hospital separately. Her rules would be tough to abide by in the ER. But not impossible. And he was happy with those odds.

CHAPTER SIX

AVERY SIGNED OVER her young patient and, though she hadn't been aware of holding her breath, finally released it as Rocky, who was pushing the child's wheelchair, managed to get her and her parents to laugh as they headed to the oncology ward.

Cancer patients weren't exactly regulars in the ER, but they did come in from time to time and ones like these, little girls who were struggling for breath, riddled with pain… It took its toll unless you shut down part of yourself like she had after April died.

Being too involved was why she'd chosen to switch to emergency medicine. Move 'em in. Move 'em out. Didn't mean she didn't give patients the same standard of care she'd want herself. A top-rate one. It was more…there wasn't time to get attached. Hear their life story. Meet all of their family enough times to know who made peach pie and who couldn't cook for a hill of beans. Who read novels to the patient when they were too tired to do it themselves. Who watched films and constantly whispered spoilers. Who wiped the patient's face clean of sputum and grime whenever they were sick, held their hair, shaved it when it started falling out, all of the things that made saying goodbye to a person so much harder than if you'd only known them for ninety minutes or less. St. Dolly's didn't short shrift their patients, but they'd rather see the backside of a treated patient than the anxious expression of someone walking in. Which was why when the electronic doors opened and Avery's former singing teacher walked in, her heart nearly tore in two.

Bonnie Chisholm was about as close to a second mom as April and Avery had had. Not that they'd needed one. Theirs was great. But Bonnie had seen something in the two of them and nurtured it as if they were her own. When singing lessons were a "twice a week" thing in Avery's life, she felt she'd known everything about Bonnie. One glimpse told her she'd been wrong to stop seeing her. Their friendship hadn't just been about singing. It had been long enough and strong enough to be founded in love. In friendship. Friendship that shouldn't have been dropped like a hot potato.

Bonnie, like Avery, had changed since April's

death. Whereas Avery had lost weight, Bonnie had gained it. A lot of it. She was trying to decide whether to rush over to help or hide when a familiar scent filled her nostrils. Pine and beeswax.

Her bottom gave a reflexive wiggle, preparing itself to receive an elicit stroke and her tummy began to form a whorl of delight.

"Hey, there." Carter's voice did what it always did. Tickled some warmth into that sweet triangle between her legs.

Dammit! Not right now.

"What's wrong?" he asked.

She frowned and felt her jaw twitch. How did he manage to appear exactly when she didn't want him to?

Moments like these when she wanted a hug more than anything.

Allowing herself a Carter hug was not going to happen. They were too soothing. Too much like feeling safe and protected. The kind of security that would've been impossible not to want to feel forever.

She'd made the mistake of feeling that with her adoptive family and even some boyfriends, but all of that stood as proof that she wasn't someone people stuck around for.

Carter, at least, had the honesty to say as much up front. Their affair had an end date, something which she had to remind herself of after every time they made love.

Since she was going to be back on her own at some point, sorting herself out when she was hurting was the only option.

But Carter didn't know that the patient walking through the door knew just about everything. He didn't know that when Avery hadn't been able to sing at her own sister's funeral, Bonnie had done it for her. Stood up in front of everyone, put her arm around a voiceless Avery, and put music to all the feelings eating Avery up inside. And that was the last time they'd seen one another.

Nor did he know that Avery needed three seconds to put a clamp on her emotions before she talked to or about Bonnie and he'd caught her two seconds too early.

"What's going on?" He nudged her with his elbow. "You're being weird. Even for you."

Glare. "Nothing."

"Liar."

"So? What business is it of yours?" she snapped, knowing she shouldn't have, but work was not the place to discuss why her insides were tying up in a knot so tight her blood flow was feeling threatened. Maybe this whole "friends with benefits" plan was stupid. She didn't even tell Lia this kind of stuff. So what was she going to do? Deposit all her broken hopes and dreams in Carter, then watch him walk away so she could be a clean slate? She was pretty sure life didn't work like that.

She looked at Bonnie again. Really looked at her. And her heart sank, finally propelling her into doing something.

She swept her tablet off the counter and grabbed an empty wheelchair for Bonnie, who was clearly struggling. For breath, with her balance, even her focus, and she'd only got a handful of steps inside the waiting room. Heart attack? TIA?

"Bonnie? Hey, there. It's Avery. Avery Whittacker. Why don't you take a seat, here? Let me help you get checked in."

Bonnie all but collapsed into the chair. She was petite in height and had always been plump, but she was definitely on the wrong side of overweight now. As Avery helped ease her feet onto the footrest, she saw that Bonnie's ankles weren't just chunkier than normal, they were swollen. Painfully so.

"Bonnie?"

A man with jet-black hair and an aura of Johnny Cash ran into the ER. He dropped down on one knee in front of her without so much as a glance at Avery. "Bonnie, honey. I told you to wait on the bench outside for me."

"It was cold, Levi. And I told you, you fuss too much."

"You think I'm not gonna fuss over the woman I love? You got another think coming." He turned to Avery. "You a doctor? This here ornery ol' hellcat needs some tending to."

Despite the gravity of the moment, Avery's lips twitched. She'd called Bonnie many things over the years, most of them loving, but never a *hellcat*.

"Bonnie, what's brought you here today?"

"It's my legs."

"So, no chest pain?"

Bonnie shook her head.

Avery pressed her fingers to Bonnie's wrist as she asked, "No discomfort in either of your arms? Back? Neck? Jaw? Stomach?" She got a decisive headshake to each of these. "You seemed a bit short of breath when you came in."

"Avery, darlin'. If you're wondering if I'm having a heart attack, you can stop," snipped Bonnie. "I already said. It's my legs." She tugged up the hem of her long velvet skirt to reveal two very swollen legs with a handful of very prominent varicose veins.

"Let's get you checked in."

Bonnie grabbed her wrist. "I've got lessons tonight, darlin'. Tell me it won't take long."

Avery would've loved to, but sometimes varicose veins indicated a much more serious vascular condition. Which meant Bonnie would need to see her bestie, Dr. Lia Costa, if she was right. She could already imagine drawing a music note on Bonnie's wrist, so that Lia would know straightaway that Bonnie was Avery's patient.

"You know what?" Bonnie started to push up and out of the chair. "I think I'm feeling better. You folk look real busy, so it might be best if I headed on back home."

Two age-worn hands pressed down on her shoulders. "Oh, no, you don't!"

"Levi West! Since when do you think you get to tell me what to do?"

"Since the moment I laid eyes on you and knew I'd love you forever," Levi humphed. He turned to Avery. "I take it you know Bonnie."

Avery nodded. Explaining why she knew Bonnie wasn't necessary. You only knew Bonnie for one reason: singing.

"Well, then. You'll know she's stubborn as a mule. Would you check her in, please? Her legs have been hurting something fierce lately." He rattled off a few incidents when they'd gone out and Bonnie had been unable to finish getting from here to there. "Not in any comfort anyway. Probably woulda crawled if I hadn't insisted upon us getting a taxi."

Avery started tapping on her tablet, finding the role reversal strange. Bonnie had always looked after her and April. Caught their stray notes and righted them. Soothed their egos when a gig didn't go to plan. Paraded around like a peacock when it did.

"Need a hand with anything here?"

"Well, hello there, young man. Yes. Yes, you can." Levi shook Carter's hand. "If you can help convince the love of my life that it's time she had some *professional help*, I'd be grateful."

"I told you, Levi. My grandmother's poultice was working just fine."

There were sores? Now, that was concerning. Not that the other factors weren't, but...

Despite Avery's annoyance that Carter had come over when she very clearly hadn't wanted him there, they exchanged a knowing look. Sometimes self-care was great. Other times... maybe not so much. And even though she hadn't seen Bonnie since the day they laid April to rest, the thought of losing Bonnie on top of everyone else felt like a razor blade against her heart.

"Why don't we take you on over to number seven?" Carter gave the woman Avery had gone all tetchy about a wink and a country smile and, despite Avery's scowl, took over wheelchair duty. Something had passed through Avery's eyes when she'd finally met his that he hadn't liked seeing. Fear. "Once we get you all settled on a proper exam chair, Avery can check out your stats and we'll see how we go from there."

The scowl twitched into something a bit closer to concession.

He could tell Avery wasn't pleased he'd joined them, but unfortunately he also knew what it was like treating people you knew well. Too well, in his case. From what he'd overheard, Avery wasn't her usual composed professional self. If emotions were going to get in the way of any sort of urgent treatment, it was his job to intervene. It was also his job as Avery's secret boyfriend not to step too soundly on his secret girlfriend's toes. He steered the wheelchair toward the exam area, well aware that Avery was boring two glare holes into his back as he did.

"Right, then." He gave Bonnie a nod once they were in place. "Why don't we get you up here on the exam chair?"

Despite ample protests, Avery and Carter managed to get Bonnie up and out of the chair.

Now that they'd achieved that, something in Avery clicked in and she became the professional nurse practitioner he admired on a daily basis. Whether she was doing it for his benefit or for her own, to calm her nerves, was hard to tell, but there was definitely a brick loose in her foundation this afternoon.

"Okay, Bonnie." Avery held up her tablet while Carter washed his hands and pulled on some exam gloves. "We'll rattle through these, so we can get you in and out of here, all right?"

"Now, that's more like it, darlin'. At least some one is paying attention to what *I* want." Bonnie glared at her significant other. Carter hadn't noticed a ring, but not everyone wore them. He would. If he made that sort of commitment to a woman, he'd want the whole world to know he was taken. His brain stop-started itself and did a little regroup. What the hell? He'd never once thought about himself as the marrying type, and now he was already committing to wearing a ring so the whole world would know.

"Name?"

"What are you wasting your breath asking me that for, Avery Whittacker?"

Avery pursed her lips and said out loud as she typed, "Bonita Sunbeam Chisholm."

Bonnie took umbrage. "Avery! You know how I feel about my full name."

"And you know how I feel about taking care of yourself."

"Bonita Sunbeam?" whooped Levi, covering up Avery's snafu. "I never knew that." He gave Bonnie's arm a squeeze. "Darlin', you just keep getting better and better."

"Deader and deader more like." Bonnie pursed her lips at him, then glared at Avery. "Go on. You said you were going to wrap this up."

To Carter's surprise, Avery became even more brisk. Bonnie was a singing teacher who had been giving a lesson, and when the time had come to show her student out, she'd struggled to get her legs to bring her to the door to wave goodbye as she normally would. Avery didn't comment on the incident, just nodded. Together they whipped through Bonnie's vital signs, which weren't great, but she wasn't having a heart attack, so that was something. When they'd finished, to Carter's surprise, Avery said to him, "You seem to be on top of things, Dr. Booth. Why don't I leave you all to it for the rest of the exam?"

"No!" Bonnie shook her head. "Avery, I know this is uncomfortable but I'm as humiliated as you are hurt, so I'd be grateful if you'd stay."

He watched Avery digest and swallow down

the request. What the hell had happened between these two women?

Avery said nothing, but she stayed.

"Pull up your skirt, honey," Levi gently en-
couraged Bonnie. "Show 'em what you showed
me."

Bonnie's bright blue eyes flashed with irritation, but she conceded.

Carter bit back a whistle. This poor woman's
legs had been through the wars. She had a fair
number of varicose veins, a couple of which
were inflamed and one or two of them, at a
glance, had caused breaks in the skin.

Bonnie saw where they were looking. "That's
not what you think it is."

Levi jumped in. "She says it's her and the
cat getting into a scrap, but I'm not convinced."

Because Avery wasn't doing anything, Carter
took the lead questioning Bonnie as to whether
or not she'd received any treatment for them
before.

"No. Like I said, whenever I've had a bump
or a break in the skin, I've used my grandmother's poultice as a cure-all. That, along with
some rest and elevation, seems to do the trick."
She gave them all a supercilious look. "I can
read the internet same as everyone else."

Carter refrained from his thoughts on self-diagnosis via the internet. "Elevation's good. As is rest. What's in this poultice of yours?"

"Bread, linseed, baking soda and mustard. You mix in a bit of water, mush it all up and then I heat it in the microwave. Sometimes if it's throbbing, I throw in some honey. Nature's own preservative."

Carter nodded and took a look at the skin breaks. They were clean. No infection. Even so, the scientist in him really wished she'd let him flush them out and put some sterile gauze pads and adhesive bandages on them. But her vitals weren't off the charts, the varicose veins were more stage two or three than stage four when he would definitely be suggesting that it was time for medical intervention. But…keeping patients in against their will wasn't his modus operandi unless their condition demanded it. Which, in Bonnie's case, it didn't. Even so, concern niggled at him. Her blood pressure was high. Her oxygen saturation levels weren't great. Not low enough—or not high enough, in the case of carbon dioxide—to warrant keeping her in for observation unless she insisted, but she seemed more intent on getting out than staying in.

"Tell me, Miss Bonnie—" he sat down on a stool next to her so they were at eye level with one another "—how's your diet?"

"Too full of fat and sugar. I think you know

that." She pointed at her generous proportions. "I know, I know. I will start another diet today."

"Try not thinking of it as a diet, more as a—"

"Lifestyle choice," she finished for him. "This ain't my first rodeo, Doc. My lifestyle choice involves baked goods and fried eggs, so...don't worry. I'll regroup. Throw a few carrot sticks into the mix. Is that it?"

"Not just yet."

She huffed in irritation and crossed her arms over her chest.

"Do you cross your legs a lot?"

"Her ankles," Levi answered for her. "She's the daintiest little thing. Always crosses her legs at the ankles like a dancer."

"Do you ever wear compression stockings?"

Bonnie nodded. "Most of the time actually. I got a pair on a flight to New Orleans once for a concert. They were all in the wash today, so I didn't bother. Probably why I ended up in this mess. Look—" she gave Carter's hand a pat "—you seem like a nice young man, but I've got another student coming in a bit, so if you don't mind, I'll just get out of your hair."

Carter wasn't happy with this. He began explaining how varicose veins, particularly ones in the state hers were in could not only lead to further complications but could be indicative of much more serious problems. Blood clots. Embolisms. Strokes. Any number of things that, if left untreated, could be fatal.

"Indicative, schmindicative. I'm not interested."

"I am," Levi said. "Do you have any pamphlets or things I could have to read up on this?"

"Absolutely."

Avery was out of the cubicle and back with an enormous handful of instructional leaflets quick as a flash. She pointedly explained to Levi about the warning signs to look for when peripheral arterial disease flared up. "It's also known as window shopper's disease."

"Oh, she gets that. Can't stop outside more than one or two stores without needing a sit down."

"Levi West, will you please stop giving away my intimate information."

"It's not intimate if telling these good folk is going to keep you alive longer," Levi protested. "I only just met you, woman. I'm not going to let you go that easily."

Carter smiled. He wished he had half of this guy's guts. He'd found someone he liked and he was going for it. Carter had, too, but was letting fear do half his decision-making. Not exactly the bravest path to follow, but it was the smartest. The most practical anyway.

Okay it was stupid, but Avery didn't seem all that keen on letting him into her life, either, so…birds of a feather and all that.

"Right." Bonnie had clearly had enough. "I think elevating in this fancy chair of yours has done the trick. Time to go."

Carter managed to win a handful of extra minutes. He wanted to put a few stitches into her open wounds and give them some proper dressing. "I would definitely get yourself a couple extra pairs of those compression socks, as they seem to be doing the trick for you, but next time you and your cat have a tussle and the skin starts weeping on your legs, come on in. I'd like to have a second look. Not that I'm saying anything against your grandmother's poultice, you hear?"

"Better not be." Bonnie glowered and then, as Carter carried on wrapping the gauze around her calf, she abruptly turned her attention to Avery. "I know you don't want me to bring it up, but I've just got to ask. When are you getting back up on a stage?"

All of the blood drained from Avery's face. Carter kept on working on Bonnie's legs, but he knew Avery knew he was soaking up every word of this one-sided exchange.

Bonnie continued, "You are every bit as talented as April was, young woman. I know you never thought that, but it's true."

Avery chewed on her lips but said nothing, which seemed to suit Bonnie just fine because she wasn't done yet. "It's a big talent wasted. I understand you needed your time to grieve, and you've had that now."

"Honey!" Levi, who'd clearly heard the background to Avery's story, intervened. "You know as well as I that there's no time limit on these things. Only life."

"Precisely," Bonnie minced. "Which is why she needs to get that cute little tush of hers back in for some lessons, then up on a stage."

Avery put on a smile that didn't come even close to lighting up those dark eyes of hers. "I'm really pleased to see you have someone in your life looking out for you, Bonnie." She switched her gaze to Levi's. "You make sure you bring her back in here if you suspect any trouble."

He said he would and then, without so much as a goodbye, Avery left.

Later—much later, in fact, because the rest of the shift felt like a game of dodge 'em when it came to nailing Avery to the spot for more than two seconds—Carter finally managed to corner her in the small office where they all did paperwork. He sat down in a wheeled chair and whirled hers around so she was facing him. She did not look impressed. He didn't much care. "What was all that back there with Bonnie? About you singing and everything?"

"I could've handled that patient on my own."

"That wasn't what I asked. And for the record, no one said you couldn't."

"Then why'd you go busting in like you did?"

"Because you looked upset."

"Taking care of me is not your job."

He winced. He'd heard that before. Usually during visiting hours down at one county jail or another after he'd drawn up a list of symptoms for the warden to distribute to all the guards. But looking after Avery was different. It wasn't an obligation. It was a choice. And he wanted to do it. The same way Levi wanted to look after Bonnie. Somewhere, down beneath all of the emotional scar tissue he'd built up over the years, Carter knew there was a man who could love a woman the right way. Completely. With all his heart. He just didn't know if he could get there anymore. So, yeah. Avery was right. Even though he didn't want her to be.

He tried to force the depth of emotion churning away inside him out of his voice. Feelings couldn't play a role in this discussion. "I take it she was your singing teacher?"

"You can also take it that it is none of your business." There was a bite to her tone.

"Hey." He tried to give her hand a squeeze, but she yanked it away before he could. "I thought we were going to be friends as well as…erm…enjoying the benefits."

Avery opened her mouth, obviously poised to let him know what a ridiculous idea that had been, then stopped herself. "You want to know what it'd be like being friends with me? Knowing all about me?"

"Yes, I do." He meant it and from the look on her face, she was grateful for it.

"Well, tough. What you see is what you get." And then she walked out of the room.

CHAPTER SEVEN

AVERY AND LIA each heaved huge sighs of relief as two very large margaritas and an enormous mortar bowl full to the brim of freshly pounded guacamole arrived in front of them. Steam was still coming off the basket of salted tortilla chips. And the tang of the vinegary salsa cut through it all.

Bliss.

Guac and Talk night with Lia was sacred and tonight was no different.

Well. Maybe a little different. For some insane reason, she'd actually considered pouring out her soul to Carter earlier today. Maybe it had been seeing Bonnie. Maybe it had been that glint of pain she'd seen in his eyes when she'd refused him access to her past. Maybe she'd just been tired of holding it all in, but…she hadn't given him or herself a chance to find out.

"You look like you've got a secret," Lia said. Not pushing, not pressing, just witnessing.

Avery smirked because admitting the truth probably would've made her cry.

You wanted to talk and cry with Carter. Why not Lia?

She made herself absorb the thought. She guessed with Carter the writing was already on the wall. He'd be leaving eventually so if he was repulsed by her outpouring of emotion, it didn't matter. The truth was she didn't know if she needed a quiet little sob or a month of ugly cries. The latter was a very strong possibility and at this point in her life she'd lost enough people, so she wasn't about to do anything that might push Lia away. If keeping some things secret and conversation light meant her friendship with Lia could stay as it was that was what she'd do.

They each took long sips of their margaritas and then had a few dunks of guacamole before Lia asked, "Would this secret have anything to do with that sexy cowboy who turned out to be an ER surgeon?"

Avery snorted, grateful Lia's take on things veered away from less comfortable topics. "Maybe?"

Lia laughed. "I'm taking it that *maybe* means *definitely* in this case."

Avery gave up any pretense of being coy. "He's the most delicious man I have ever, *ever* been with." She hadn't been with many, but still. Nashville was full to the seams with eye candy.

"Glad to see you're finally letting yourself have some fun."

Avery squirmed. It was fun. But it was also real in a way she couldn't quite describe. Time to change the subject. "How was your day? Lots of surgeries?"

"Uh-uh." Lia wagged a finger at her. "No, you don't. We're not changing the topic that quickly."

"What's there to know? He's scrumptious. We're having a good time. End of story."

Lia pursed her lips. "Avery Whittacker, you know as well as I do that you are not someone who just hops into bed with the nearest piece of edible man cake."

"Is that what the cool kids are calling it these days?" Avery laughed. "Man cake?"

"Candy. Whatever. The point is, I know you're picky. I also know you haven't so much as looked at a man since…" They both knew since when. She'd been dumped and then her sister had died. "If you're canoodling with this guy after a considerable hiatus in that department, you must see something special in him."

She did. She saw a lot of things. And none of them visible to the naked eye. He had a huge heart. He was kind. Loyal. The human form of emotional scaffolding if ever she wavered—which she had this afternoon—and she had no doubt that he was the same solid rock filled with perspective and lack of judgment for his sister, too. He looked after others before he looked after himself. If that was a flaw, it was one of his only ones. And it wasn't exactly a reason to kick him out of bed.

His inability to put down roots was his secret, and definitely not hers to tell.

Not that she didn't struggle with it. But she got it. Blood being thicker than water and all that.

Besides, she'd agreed to the expiration date for their friendship with benefits, so the way she was looking at it, she might as well keep him in the bed he'd short-sheeted.

Lia was still waiting for an answer, so Avery forced herself to smile and say, "He's great. It's early days. Too soon to make predictions of that nature. Speaking of love lives. How's yours, Lia?"

Her friend lifted up her glass and hooted. "Touché, my friend. Touché."

They both knew it hadn't exactly been on fire. Intimacy was tricky for Lia, and in the same way Lia knew to back off from Avery's sore subjects, Avery knew to do the same for her. "Now. Are you going to tell me how your day was or do I have to drag it out of you?"

Cassidy squinted at Carter as she munched her way through the spicy hot cheese puffs he'd bought from the vending machine. Her favorite. "You look different."

He gave his jaw a scrub and feigned no knowledge of anything being different about him. Externally, she was wrong. Still the same ol' unshaven scrubs-wearing straight-from-the-hospital big brother she'd always known. Internally, she was spot on. He'd crossed a line into rocky emotional terrain and wasn't 100 percent sure he'd made the wisest choice.

Being there for someone meant loving them despite their faults. Like he did with Cassidy.

He wasn't sure he knew Avery well enough to even know her faults. Privacy maybe? Not that that was much of a crime. But the Avery he made love to was a totally different woman to the one he worked with. And the version of her when they'd been treating Bonnie, the singing teacher? Again. Totally different.

He'd run into Bonnie's boyfriend in the waiting room a while later and, unsolicited, Levi had colored in a few of the blank spots in the portrait he was building of her.

This is where it stood now: strong, passionate beautiful woman who was completely on her own after her sister's death; grandparents gone to natural causes; parents who'd lost their minds with grief and up and left as if adopting Avery hadn't meant the same thing to them as it had to her. He knew grief did savage things to people, but he'd been so mad when he'd heard that part of the story, he could've spit nails.

He'd wanted to jump in his truck, drive across the country, find her parents, hitch their mobile home up to his truck and drag them back here to be with their daughter. The one still living with as much pain as they were.

Hearing her story—or part of it anyway— had dragged him through the anguish of losing his own parents afresh. First, his dad to sickle cell and then, as Cassidy liked to put it, their mother of heartbreak. His father's last words to him still rung in his head. *You're the man of the house now, Carter. You make sure you look after your mother and your sister same as I tried to.* His mother had died less than a year after his father, so that had been a massive fail.

The only way he'd been able to make money at that point, as a teenaged boy, was to ride bulls like his daddy had done before him. His dad had done it for the same reason Cassidy stole stuff. To feel alive. Lucky for Carter, he was good at it. It paid for the apartment he and his much younger sister lived in. His med school fees. And everything in between. He'd stuffed away a lot of his winnings for a rainy day, but he'd seen enough guys on the circuit suffer life-changing injuries to step away from it as soon as he could.

Getting on that mechanical bull on New Year's Eve had been his first ride in years and years. Which meant Avery had made one hell of an impact on him and already he knew walking away from her would be harder than walking away from prize riding. So, yeah. He was different. Didn't mean he was going to admit to it.

"Same ol' me," he finally said. "How're they treating you in here?"

She gave him a big smile, her lips coated with artificial cheese powder. "It's just like the Ritz, big brother." The smile dropped away and now, as she turned into the light, he saw the shadow of a black eye. She clocked him noticing. "I'm fine. Don't get all fussed like you normally do. It's all fine."

"How's the clinic?"

She shrugged in that careless way of hers. "Dunno. Haven't been there yet."

"Why not?"

"Been in solitary." She glared at him, daring him to comment.

Carter bit back a remonstration. She'd only been here two weeks and already she'd managed to be in a fight and earn some time in solitary. Fan-freaking-tastic.

"You always said to make an impression." She popped the last corn puff into her mouth and began to lick the orange powder off her fingers.

"Yeah, a *good* one, Cassidy." He was about to say he was going to have a chat with the prison doctor when she looked up at him and he saw something in her eyes that caught him off guard. Regret. She'd never once expressed remorse at her actions, but if he was feeling a sea change in his life, maybe she was, too. He leaned in but the movement made her blink and when she opened her eyes again, it was gone.

She had the same green eyes as his. As their dad's. A man whose advice he could use right about now. He'd always been better with Cassidy than he had.

It was hard to forgive the eighteen-year-old version of himself for being so mad at her when she'd "enjoyed" her first stint in juvy. Their dad had only been dead a few months and their mother had checked out emotionally the day he'd died, so the fact that Cassidy had gone off the rails hadn't been much of a surprise. But he'd had his head too buried in books and his body too wrapped up in testing his own mortality in the bull ring to pay her the right kind of attention.

Bad call.

He should've been better. Which was why pulling the plug on relationship after relationship had been easy. Until now.

He scrubbed his hands through his hair, letting his nails dig into his skull. He wanted to feel Cassidy's pain. See the world the way she did. Understand why the hell breaking the law gave her the high it did. But he knew deep down he never could. He'd been lucky in the gene pool game. She hadn't. Her disease was a time bomb, relentlessly ticking away, and if her number was up when their dad's had been up…she only had about ten years left. So why the hell was spending it locked up the better option to being free?

The guard called time. Groans of disappointment mingled with sighs of relief at the handful of occupied tables around them.

"Same time next week?" he asked.

"If you're lucky." She gave him her cheekiest smile and then, with the prison guard's eyes firmly on them, they shared a quick fierce hug. They both knew it was impossible to predict if this was just a regular ol' visit or the last time they saw one another.

"Love you, sis."

Cassidy stared at him. Hard. He didn't say things like that. Not often enough anyway. She jabbed her finger at him. "Next time, you're going to tell me what's up."

He nodded and rose from the table.

"And Carter?"

"Yeah?" He braced himself for some sort of telling off.

"Love you, too." Then she whirled around and, without a backward glance, disappeared behind the bulletproof reinforced door.

He smiled and shook his head. It was the first time she'd said it back. Maybe something had shifted in that mixed-up heart of hers. And just like that, the promises he'd made to himself to let her get on with her life and deal with her problems on her own evaporated.

CHAPTER EIGHT

THE REALTOR HELD her hands out once they'd circled back to the front door and gave Avery and Carter a winning smile. "Now, if you and your husband would like some time alone in the house, I'm happy to go make some calls. There's heat in my car and my hands are near enough frozen."

Avery was about to interject, explain that Carter was most definitely not her husband, and that she wasn't even sure why she'd invited him along, but he got there first.

"That'd be great." He slung an arm over her shoulders and pulled her in for an awkward side cuddle.

The realtor opened the front door and wagged her finger. "No hanky-panky before we get your signature on a contract, hear?"

Avery squirmed. Carter laughed and said something about how there were no guarantees on that front. Avery gave him a look. She could've guaranteed it.

She hadn't wanted him to come, but he'd met her after her shift at work with a bag of take-out barbecue and a flimsy excuse about having ordered too much. He'd been to see his sister and, though he didn't spell it out, the visit had obviously unsettled him, so, like an idiot, she'd taken him up on his suggestion that he come along.

She looked around. Maybe it was a good idea having someone who wasn't as invested in the place as she was have a look. The place wasn't quite as robust as she'd remembered it. The wraparound porch floorboards weren't just creaky; they had some give in them. The shingled roof looked like it would need replacing in the not too distant future. It would take time and money and most of all love to turn this place into a home. Panic set in that she was short on all three.

Perhaps buying this place was a pipe dream she'd clung to. A means of keeping just a bit of her sister alive. "So?" She heard the false bravura in her voice and did her best not to crumble under the weight of it. "What do you think?"

"Five Acre Farm, huh?" Carter's fingers were

hooked on his hips and his gaze appraising the place as if he actually cared.

She could hear the defensiveness in her voice when she answered, "I guess whoever named it didn't have much of an imagination."

"Nothing wrong with calling a spade a spade," Carter said, his eyes catching with hers.

What did *that* mean? He was the one who'd just pretended they were married to the realtor.

Before she could pursue it, he asked, "How far out from the hospital is it?"

"Thirty minutes without traffic." Twenty to her sister's school, she added silently. They'd done the timings a few times before April had had to quit her job and then, eventually, stay at the hospital. But Avery had taken to driving back and forth like therapy. None of which had bought the house, restored it and got her sister living the life they'd dreamed in it, but...

Her shoulders began to wilt. This was an awful idea. And she hated having Carter here to witness it.

Carter cleared his throat. "I think the setting is one in a million, but the house itself..." He turned the kitchen tap on, then off when the water ran brown. "Definitely a fixer-upper. It'll take a lot of work to get this place where you want it."

Her instinct was to bristle, fight back, but

he was right. The house had sat empty for five years now. Unlived in. Unloved. Falling apart in bits it probably shouldn't be. Her eyes lit on the stone fireplace in the center of the living room. Each stone carried up from the riverbed by whoever had built the place. And just like that, she fell in love with it again. You didn't get that sort of touch in a new build. That sort of commitment. It was the type of commitment and care she'd want in a relationship, but obviously wasn't destined to get. So…maybe pouring all the love she had to give that no one seemed to want into restoring the house would be the next best thing. Right?

Carter appeared beside her. Ran a finger along the stones in the fireplace. "What kind of life had you pictured living here?"

Avery blinked away her surprise. How did he do that? It was like he'd tapped straight into her brain, her heart, her gut. Telling him didn't feel like giving anything away he didn't already know.

They walked and she talked.

She looked around the house that she had once imagined living in with her sister. They'd each earmarked one of the bedrooms upstairs. The third bedroom was to be for guests. They'd planned to hang old quilts on the walls, fill the beds and sofas with throw cushions galore and the whole house with so much laughter.

"So what's the plan now?" Carter asked. "Since that won't happen apart from the quilts and cushions."

"You don't pull punches, do you?" She was really regretting telling him her origin story.

He held up his hands. "I may be a lot of things, but a realist seems to be the most useful."

"Yeah? Well, maybe some optimism would help you be a bit happier!" she spat back.

"Is that your trick, Avery? Why you're so full of laughter and joy? Why you work in the ER instead of oncology? Optimism?"

His voice hadn't raised, and his tone hadn't changed from the same amiable way he'd asked about whether or not there was a well or a water main for the house. He was doing what a good friend would. Questioning her motives. Didn't mean it didn't hurt.

She glowered, but deep down knew he was right. So, as painful as it was, she pushed the pictures of the life she'd planned on living here with April to the side and imagined herself living here on her own.

Instantly, it felt too big. She glanced at Carter who was tapping on walls and knocking on beams or struts, or whatever the things that held up walls were called, and allowed herself a glimpse of another life. One with a husband and children. A couple of horses. And a puppy, of course.

The images flew into place so quickly she knew they were too perfect to believe so she forced herself to blink them away and, though it was as cold and miserable inside as outside, she suddenly felt claustrophobic in there. She headed to the back door.

All the land that came with the house was out back. A handful of acres surrounded by woodland where she'd once imagined having a couple of her granddad's rescue horses. They'd all literally moved on to greener pastures now. Some in heaven. Some in Kentucky where they'd found another horse rescue center.

"What's this?" Carter pointed at an outbuilding. The bottom half might've been a workshop or a storeroom for horse gear, garden equipment. But the upstairs…

Avery bit the inside of her cheek. She and April had pictured it as a studio. Not necessarily for recording, but a place where they could play music and sing without disturbing the neighbors. They weren't too close to the next house, another few acres and more woodland acted as a buffer, but April was one of those women who thought of absolutely everything. She was considerate right down to her core. *An earth angel* her mother used to sing whenever April brought home another bird with a broken wing or an orphaned kitten or a child she saw getting picked on at school. The fact she'd ended up a kindergarten teacher had been no surprise to anyone.

"Is that your favorite corner of the building?"

Avery gave Carter a hard stare. "It happens to be a perfectly delightful corner."

"Oh, yeah? Even the mouse hole there in the wall?"

She made herself actually look at the corner that, as Carter had clocked, she'd been blindly staring at. Yup. Sure enough, there was a mouse hole. He leaned on the banister that led to the upstairs annex. It gave under his weight.

"You break it, you buy it," they said in tandem. Then laughed. Some of the weirdness of seeing this house together disappeared as the sound of their laughter melded together like voices in a duet. Just the way she'd pictured it.

Could her friendship with Carter be the thing she needed to feel whole again? To remind her of the woman she'd once been? Or, better yet, the one she'd one day hoped to become?

She looked at him hard. What did Carter Booth bring to her life?

They had really good sex. He made her laugh. He also made her mad. Made her think. Made her want to be a better version of herself and that was no bad thing.

Carter wanted to know her. He couldn't meet the version of her she'd once been. She was finally figuring out that she'd been so lost in her grief she'd made no time to consider the woman she'd become. A shell of a human fixated on buying this tumbledown house.

She had her work, of course. She loved that. But apart from her friendship with Lia, it was as if she'd put every other element of herself in the deep freeze. It'd have to thaw one day. That's how life worked.

She realized it was important to see what it felt like for someone to know both the old Avery and whoever the heck the new Avery was. It felt terrifying, but something deep in her belly told her Carter would be careful with her, whatever happened.

"Bonnie, that patient from yesterday," she said. "The one in the ER I got all cranky about. She was my singing teacher."

Carter nodded. "I figured as much."

"She was also my sister's singing teacher."

Carter nodded, taking a step back as if instinctively knowing she needed a bit more space in which to let her story unfold. "This building, the house, the stable…it was going to be where all our dreams would come true."

The corners of his mouth shifted into a soft smile. "That sounds nice."

She nodded. "I didn't think it'd be so…so…"

"So much of a wreck?" he filled in for her.

She nodded.

He leaned against a wall after checking it for durability. "I thought you'd been saving for a deposit for the place? Surely you've been in it before?"

She shook her head.

His eyes bugged out a little bit.

"I know." She waved her hands. "I know. I just… We'd been in here years back, April and I. Before we could afford it, so we only snuck onto the property and peeked in the windows and such. It had seemed a little unloved then, but it hadn't mattered. We had our grandparents, our parents, all our friends— April couldn't pass a person without becoming friends with 'em—so the whole place probably could've been leaning halfway to the ground and we wouldn't have cared. We just loved it."

"The way a person loves a scruffy homeless puppy?" His "hound dog" eyes met hers and something flared between them as they met and meshed. Something that went beyond friendship.

A thought bashed into her like a wrecking ball.

Was opening the door to her past also opening up the possibility of loving him?

Heaven knew she'd loved being held in his arms at night. Their bodies seemed to have known one another for years. Instinctively able to elicit pleasure. And safety. Despite his "alpha male" exterior, the man loved a cozy cuddle under the comforter in the morning. The heat of their bodies merging as one. The limbs. Their breath. Their heartbeats.

But puppies—and by puppies, she meant Carter—were difficult. They demanded attention. Wanted things their way. They ate your favorite boots. Tore up the sofa cushions. Wormed their way into your heart in the blink of an eye without anyone having much of a say in the matter. So much of the last few years had been out of her control—she wasn't sure she was up for it. Not holding the reins of her own life.

Was there a middle ground? Did love even work like that?

No. She didn't think it did. Her sister hadn't had a choice in "leaving." Carter Booth did. Sort of. And it was that gray area that made fully opening up her heart to him a no-brainer. She simply couldn't do it.

Carter felt like he was watching someone physically mash themselves through an emotional wringer. This house wasn't just a house to Avery. It was meant to have been her future. He wasn't going to preach to her, but she knew as well as he did that *things* don't make a future, people do. Even so…maybe Avery had to work through her so-called dream plan in order to learn that lesson firsthand. Put in the inevitable blood, sweat and tears this place would require.

Though the price wasn't exorbitant, it was still a lot of money to put down on a dream that would never come true. A dream that had plenty of potential to become a nightmare.

He had enough money saved up that he could buy it straight-out, but this was Avery's thing. She wanted to put her hard-earned money down. Her graft into buffing up those hardwood floors. Dirty up her clothes painting all those walls into a pretty series of pastels or whatever it was she had planned.

Yeah, he saw that. He also couldn't tear himself out of the picture. Not fully anyway.

"You know," he said, pushing himself off and away from the wall with a booted foot. "I don't know if I've mentioned it, but I do know my way around a hammer and nail." He gave her a wink.

He watched as she rearranged her features into something akin to disinterest, but he'd seen the hope light up her eyes. "Oh, really?"

"Yes, ma'am." He tipped the corner of his Stetson at her. "I partly paid my way through college by using these." He held out his hands. It was what he'd turned to after he'd started seeing X-rays and MRIs of what really happened inside a man who strapped himself to a bucking bull.

She blushed a little as she said, "There's a lot of things a man can do with his hands."

His mind instantly flashed back to the other night when he'd used them to scoop up her bare buttocks and draw her to him, so she had a little elevation to slide onto his erection. The memory began to elicit another one. He glanced around, stupidly looking for a bucket of ice water.

"I used to work on building sites."

She raised her eyebrows.

Okay. Good. She wasn't saying no. He hitched his hands onto his belt buckle and took a risk. "If you're willing, maybe I could give up that soul-sucking serviced apartment, and in exchange for a bed, I could be your handyman.

book. She knew buying this house wouldn't bring her sister back and maybe every second she spent in it would be torture. But he felt in his bones that she would learn from it. Move on in whatever way she saw best once she'd acknowledged her grief and found a way to move past it—or live with it. He sure as hell didn't know how that worked.

His brain rattled through the hundreds of conversations he and his sister had had over the years. One-way mostly. Him pleading with her to stop her reckless behavior. Begging her to settle down. Bargaining. Raging. It was like going through the five stages of grief every single time he walked through those prison doors. She wouldn't even need to get a job he'd plead. He'd support her. But she should be living her life on the outside. Freely. Happily. Not locked up and counting her days like they were numbered. Which, of course, they were.

"Hey." Avery reached out and gave his arm a squeeze. "What happened there?"

He shook his head. "Just thinking that my sister will never know something like this."

"Like what?"

"Working hard. Saving up. Trying to make a dream come true."

Avery frowned. "Do you think it's stupid? Trying to do something I was supposed to do with my sister even though I know it won't come close to the same?"

He considered his answer carefully. "As long as you know that in advance—that it won't be the same—then I don't think there is any reason why you shouldn't go for it."

A look of helplessness consumed her. "How am I even going to begin? I've had this one dream that I've clung to and—" She lifted her hands up, then let them flop down on her sides. "The place is a wreck. It's not even worth what they're asking."

"Then put in a lower offer." He did a quick calculation, gave her a number that made her blink a few times, then put his offer out again. "I'm willing to help you. If you want to look at this as a fixer-upper instead of the place you're going to live out the remains of your days, it'll make it easier. You can still love the place. Put some of that Avery Whittacker glow into it—"

She laughed. "Avery Whittacker glow?"

"Yeah." He took her hands in his and tugged her a little closer to him. "You radiate something magic. I don't know what it is exactly, but if you poured some of that into this place—" he tipped his head toward the house "—I bet you could get double what you put into it."

"And you'd help me?"

The question was a big one, because it wasn't just a matter of bringing his toolbox over and fixing some squeaky doors. Though they'd only known one another a few weeks, they already had a comfy little routine. She had a key to his apartment. They knew each other's rosters at work. When their paths crossed at "home," such as it was, they ripped one another's clothes off and set the world alight. When they were at work, they worked.

But this place? The one she'd dreamed of for years? He'd be putting an imprint on it. When he left—because that was the one thing they both knew was inevitable—he'd be part of this place. No matter how many layers of paint she put on it. He'd be there.

He looked at her and saw everything he wanted in a woman. Honest. Passionate. Keen to make a difference in the world. Right here in this community. And he wanted a bit of that stick-to-it-ness to rub off on him...

"Yes, I would, Avery. It would be my pleasure."

And probably one of the stupider things he'd agreed to do, but he wanted to help Avery and more than anything he could see buying this place was about closure. Whether she ended up living here until her end of days or until they put the final lick of paint on that gorgeous wraparound porch, it didn't matter. She'd know in her heart she'd done her best by her sister and then could move on in whatever way necessary.

The thought stung.

Yes. He'd be moving on, too. Literally. How and when were the only unanswered questions. He cleared his throat, then nodded toward the street where the real-estate agent sat out in her car. "If you want me to play hardball on the price, I'm willing to do that for you."

Avery threw a wistful look in the direction of the house, then a hopeful one at him. "Let me see your hardball face."

He showed it to her. She laughed. The next thing he knew, her hands were slipping around his waist, he was holding her in his arms and they were kissing. Soft and light, strong and deep and everything in between. It felt like they were exchanging a silent promise to be careful with one another. After all, this was Avery's dream. Not his. She was welcoming him into her world, knowing one day he'd leave. He was grateful for her trust and would do everything in his power to honor it. Not to hurt her when that day arrived and he drove away. He deepened his kisses, already missing her. Already wishing life were different.

"I thought I said no hanky-panky!"

They pulled apart and threw sheepish looks at the realtor, who beamed at the pair of them. "I take it I need to get out my sold sign?"

CHAPTER NINE

"Whistling while we work, are we?"

Avery looked up from the supplies cart she'd been reloading and grinned at her colleague Valentina, who was doing the same. "It makes the day go quicker."

Valentina raised an approving eyebrow. "I'm guessing that means there is something or some*one* worth going home to these days?"

"Some*thing*," Avery enunciated even though she was pretty sure her and Carter's efforts to keep a cap on their attraction to one another was not quite as successful as it had been a week ago.

"I got Five Acre Farm."

Valentina's face lit up. "Oh, honey. I know you had your eye on that place for a while." Her expression shifted to one of concern. "You sure you're going to be all right in that house on your own?"

Avery nodded. "I'll be fine." And somehow,

her cart and stood up. "Guess I'd better get back to it."

She could feel Valentina's eyes on her as she walked away.

"You okay?" Carter was looking at her as if her face were doing something funny.

She thought she'd been masking her feelings, but she guessed she'd made a bad show of it. "Fine."

He made a noise that made it clear he didn't believe her. She was about to tell him to back off when a huge commotion erupted in the ambulance bay.

"Right!" Dr. Chang pushed open one of the double doors with her foot. "I need you and you." She pointed at Avery and Carter. "Someone find Rocky. We're going to need his muscles."

Avery and Carter exchanged a look. A few seconds later, they weren't confused anymore.

It took Dr. Chang and six other doctors to transfer their new patient to the gurney while the paramedic rattled off the transfer information. "Brian Culpepper. Bodybuilder. Was doing warm-up bench presses when he experienced lower back pain. Was on stage preparing for competition when he experienced numbness in his inner thighs."

"I even peed my pants!" Brian yelled. "Right there in front of everyone."

Again, Avery and Carter exchanged a look. Herniated disc. For sure. If he'd lost complete control of his pelvic bowl, things were looking bad. Real bad.

"We don't need this." Dr. Chang ripped off the heat blanket that was covering him.

Despite the gravity of the injury—sometimes it required surgery—she could see Carter struggling to keep a straight face. Brian hadn't peed his pants because he didn't have any on. Underneath the heat blanket, he was wearing nothing but a tiny little sparkly gold swimsuit-type thing. Not even. Two little strings and a bit of fabric to cover up his privates.

"Get me drugs now!" Brian roared. "I want steroids. Painkillers. The lot. I have to get back to the convention center."

"Can someone call ortho!" Dr. Chang barked, ignoring the patient's demand for painkillers. She pointed at Carter. "Get him into an exam room and see how far the numbness has spread. He'll need an MRI."

"MRI's down," Carter said.

"What?" She swore under her breath. It was rare, but machines broke. Even in hospitals. "Then get him a CT scan. Whittacker. You go with him. If he has a compression of the spinal nerve roots, he's going to need to get into surgery. Can someone book a room?"

"Or…he might just need to take it easy for a couple of days and take two aspirin," Carter said pointedly.

Dr. Chang stared at him for a moment before replying. "Back pain a specialty of yours?"

Avery tensed. This was weird. Carter didn't showboat. He stayed calm and collected, but his voice was solid as a rock when he replied, "Just aware that this could be temporary pain, Doc. Nothing a bit of ice, rest and off-the-shelf painkillers wouldn't fix."

Dr. Chang gave him a quick nod. When she was called away to see to another ambulance entering the bay, Carter breathed out.

"What are you doing, man?" the patient asked. "Don't I need painkillers and surgery, like right now?"

"How old are you?" Carter asked,

"Twenty-eight."

"And is this your thing? This weight lifting?"

"It's what I want to do as long as I can do it, and then after that I'll run a gym, training others how to do it. This competition was meant to put my name on the map. Make it easier for me to get sponsorship to find my own space."

Carter nodded. It was easy enough to hear the passion in Brian's voice. The dedication.

And the disappointment that today hadn't gone to plan.

"Do you know what surgery will involve?"

Brian looked at Avery for hints. She wasn't sure where this was going so she didn't say anything. Brian crossed his huge biceps over his chest and asserted, "Surgery fixes stuff. I need surgery." He thrust one of his enormous Thor fists into the air. "I demand surgery!"

"Fair enough." Carter's tone switched from his normal congenial self to pure business. "Just so you're aware, a discectomy means a surgeon, like myself, will cut away a portion of the disc that is pressing against your nerve. I might also have to trim away some of the bone from the backside of your vertebrae to relieve pressure on the nerves. That's a laminectomy. Thing is about nerves that have been pressed on like that, they could be damaged by the surgery."

"What?"

Carter nodded. "And not just that. The surgery comes with the risk of lifelong pain, blood clots, infection, leaking spinal fluid. Shall I go on?"

Brian didn't say anything.

"On the plus side," Carter continued, uninvited, "the mortality rate for this type of surgery is real low." He nodded at the orderly pushing the gurney and then at Avery who was steering on the side opposite him. "What do you say? Shall we skip the CT altogether and just go straight to surgery?"

"No!" Brian half sat up, then collapsed back down, the gurney shuddering beneath his considerable heft. "I think I want that scan and then maybe... Do you guys have heat pads or something? Ice packs?"

Carter nodded. "We have both and we'd be happy to help you."

Once they'd got him in for a scan and were waiting for the results, Avery asked, "What was all that about? What if he does need surgery and you just freaked him out about it?"

Carter looked above her head as he spoke, as if picturing something he'd been through before. "You know how I can ride a bull?"

She did.

"Do you know why I did it?"

She did not.

"My father used to ride to feel alive."

She frowned and started connecting some dots. So...his sister's tendency to court danger to feel alive was a precedent set by their father. It didn't entirely explain Carter's motivation.

"I don't get the connection. What does bull riding have to do with Brian's desire for surgery? His symptoms are worrying."

Carter's green eyes flared. "So is paralysis and spending the rest of your already limited life in a wheelchair if you've had unnecessary surgery."

Oh.

The penny dropped.

Carter's father had had surgery courtesy of a "too quick to react" ER doctor.

How awful. No wonder he'd gone into emergency medicine. She felt the doors to her heart nudge open even wider. Not falling in love with this man was hard!

He tipped his head toward the scans, then pointed out a blurry bit. "It's impossible to read the extent of the damage with the swelling. When that goes down, we'll have a much clearer picture. Literally and figuratively."

She got it now. Carter was always going to do the scans. The X-rays, the research. He was always going to book a surgery if he had to. But he was not going to leap to conclusions that could alter this young man's life forever. It didn't answer all her questions, though.

"So…why did you ride if your father suffered permanent damage from it?"

"Research." His eyes didn't meet hers.

No, it wasn't. He'd done it because he'd had to. But they were at work and the topic clearly touched a nerve—no pun intended—so she wasn't going to push, but…she did find his bedside manner with this patient very different from how he treated others. He needed calling on it. That or she needed to find out where it came from.

"And the way you were with Brian? Was that anger at Dr. Chang for being trigger-happy for surgery or anger at yourself for not knowing better than to intervene on your dad's behalf?"

Carter scraped his teeth across his lip and scrubbed his hand through his hair but didn't answer.

"I'm guessing a bit of both."

He held up his hands. "I'm here to fix broken people. Sometimes it works. Sometimes it doesn't. But I think a man who has a choice ought to make an educated one. Not one ruled by emotion or people in white coats being bullied by management to keep the turnover on track or bullying him into something he couldn't possibly understand without a medical degree."

And that, in a nutshell, was Carter Booth. He put himself in the shoes of his patients to figure out where they were coming from and then rammed on his surgeon's shoes and saw it from the flip side. He took into account a person's whole life. Their income, their passions, the miserable future they'd have if it were snatched away. He genuinely cared.

And it wasn't just limited to his patients.

When they were looking at her tumbledown farmhouse, he knew better than to call it a lost cause. He knew as well as she did that knocking it down and starting over would be the smartest option. But he'd seen a need in her. A need to fulfil a promise. So he'd backed her up, but also given her a way out if being there proved too painful. *Do it up, sell it on. Start over.* The solution wasn't exactly rocket science, but since she was in the weeds with all her complex emotions, he'd cleared a path for her. Then another. Let her see the big picture and asked nothing in return.

It made her heart ache for him. A man so used to giving that he never took the time to take care of himself.

She got called away before the conversation could go any further. She gave his hand a squeeze and made a silent promise to find a way to repay the kindnesses he'd shown her. Carter Booth deserved more. Much more than he was allowing himself to receive. Looked like she wasn't the only one who needed the doors to their heart being pushed open. The only question was…what would she do once she got her foot in the door? Move forward? Or retreat?

A few hours later, Carter pulled back the curtain to the bed in the observation bay and kneed a wheeled stool up to Brian's bedside.

Avery had pulled him up on his bedside manner and, though it had taken a few laps around the hospital in the snow to separate right from wrong, he knew he owed this guy an apology. It wasn't Brian's fault Carter's dad had screwed up his back, then seen a bad surgeon. Hell. The surgeon might've been great, but he knew as well as everyone surgeons weren't gods. Even if they liked to think they were. "How're you getting on with that ice pack?"

Brian feigned an expression of being semi-comatose, then grinned. "What do you know? A bit of ice, a bit of heat and not lifting up the equivalent of a polar bear does a man some good."

Carter gave him a satisfied nod. Good. He'd been right to wait. Sometimes it was that simple. Even so, the chances of injuring himself again were high, so he wanted to make sure the two of them were on the same page when this guy walked out of here. "You know masking the pain isn't going to help someone like you."

Brian squinted at him. "How so?"

"You've got enough musculature to get you by with everyday things and, of course, exercise keeps you strong. But the next time you think about picking up a heavy weight or dragging a car behind you or whatever else it is you do to get yourself ripped like that, just remember that none of it will mean a hill of beans if you've not given yourself enough rest time."

"You just said to exercise."

"I sure did. But I didn't mean training. What you're going to need to do is start from the beginning. Retrain the muscles in your back so that they move properly. I can send you some good repetition and resistance exercises to improve your stability—unilateral presses, rows, chops, lifts, side planks. That sort of thing. No twists, squats, deadlifts or overhead weight lifting."

Brian huffed out a sigh.

Through it, Carter continued, "And if you know a good physio, I'd get in touch. You'll need to see one of them before you even think of lifting anything heavier than a pencil."

Brian's features creased. "Oh, come on now, Doc. My next competition is in another week."

"Cancel it."

Brian went to protest.

Carter held up a hand. "A variation of what happened to you happened to my father."

"What happened to him?"

"He pushed it too far and spent the last good years of his life in a wheelchair."

"You serious?"

"Deadly."

"I guess I'll give the competition a miss, then."

Thank goodness. Carter had got through to him. "Do we have ourselves a deal?"

After another aggrieved sigh, they shook on it. Carter had made the impression he'd wanted to, a lasting one. If only dealing with his sister was half as easy. Instead of falling into that rat's nest, he got back to work.

Lucky for him and bad for Nashville, it appeared to be a citywide "slip and fall" day. He'd noticed the roads were icy when he drove in, but he hadn't left the hospital since the sun had risen and set. From the looks of things, the ice had hung around. Wrists, ankles, knees, shoulders, hips. The orthopedic wing was going to be full to bursting if things kept up like this.

His path didn't cross much with Avery's but when it did, she seemed a bit more lost in thought than usual. He didn't think it was anything to take personally, but sometimes you never knew what was going on in someone else's brain. After he'd set and wrapped what must've been his tenth sprained wrist of the day, he found her at the coffee station.

"Hey."

She didn't look at him. "Hey yourself."

"You okay?"

"Fine."

"Don't sound fine."

"What are you?" She finally looked at him. "The 'good mood' police?"

"Nope." He held a carton of chocolate milk he'd been drinking over her cup of coffee. "Want a dollop of something nice in that?"

She shot him a look, then finally cracked a smile. His heart softened at the sight. Funny. He hadn't realized his mood could change with hers.

"Tough day?" He put a good inch or two of chocolate milk into her coffee and she took a long satisfied drink.

"*Mmm.*" She ticked a few cases off on her fingers. "A couple more folk in from the weight-lifting thing. A few whiplash cases from fender benders, three heart attacks and one too many cases of hypothermia than should be allowed in this day and age." She pursed her lips. He'd had a couple, as well. Not good. One homeless guy and an old woman who said she couldn't afford to pay her heating bill anymore. The postman had become concerned when he saw she hadn't collected her mail in a while and hollered up at her bedroom window for about fifteen minutes before calling an ambulance. He was a good man, that postman. If more folk looked out for one another like he had—

"There was a woman in from the prison." Avery looked down, then up at him. "Not your sister. I checked the minute I heard they were bringing someone in."

She didn't say what was wrong with the woman and he didn't ask. "Thanks for checking." He cleared his throat, looked up at the ceiling, then back at Avery. "Would you ever want to meet her?"

The second the question was out, he regretted it. Why on earth would she want to meet his sister—a woman hell-bent on bringing forward her death date—when she was still clearly grieving her own sister, whose life had been cut short far too soon? Not to mention the fact it was letting someone into a part of his life that no one, apart from Cassidy, had ever been in.

"Sorry." He tried to erase the comment. "Don't answer that."

"No, I'd like to." She scrunched up her nose and gave him such a cute smile he was half tempted to give her nose a little boop. "When are you thinking?"

They decided to go that weekend. They paired their diaries, and she began to walk away. Even with a date in his phone, he still wasn't entirely convinced this was a good idea. He called after her, "You sure, now? You don't want me stripped down to my basics, hammering and nailing things?" He struck a pose. "I look extra good in a pair of jeans and nothing else."

She shot an "I'll bet you do" look over her shoulder, then shifted her smile from sexy to gentle. "Family takes precedence over worn-out floorboards."

Avery might as well have reached into his chest, grabbed his heart and popped it into her pocket for the impact the statement had. Of course, he just stood there and said something like, *Good point*, but she was right—and also a little bit not. The way his sister took precedence in his life meant he had no life. If he carried on as he was—putting his life on hold until his poor sweet sister died—he wouldn't be a dad for at least a decade, maybe more. And he wasn't sure that was the right balance of things.

Maybe it was time to break the habits of a lifetime? Put down roots and build a family of his own. He watched Avery swish her way down the hallway—she knew he was watching. He imagined what it might be like, knowing he'd see that sexy sashay every day of his life. Glancing at her hands as they shifted along her thighs and seeing the glint of an engagement ring on her finger. One he'd slipped on when he'd asked her to be his wife. His phone rang. It was the prison. He turned away from Avery so he could give his sister his full focus.

A blunt reminder that this is what family meant in his case. Total sacrifice to keep someone alive who he wasn't even sure wanted to be. As ever, he took the call, accepted the charges and walked away.

CHAPTER TEN

"Whoa!"

"Watch it, pal!"

"Someone call Security!"

"Rocky!"

Avery's instinct was to throw herself between the two men who were throwing punches right in front of her. She had properly sharp elbows when necessary. But in this scenario, she knew she didn't stand a chance. To be honest, she wasn't all that sure the spindly security guards on duty, or even Rocky, did, either. Even though his background was boxing, he was lean and not too tall and these guys were clearly from the heavyweight class at the body-building convention. She was no brain surgeon, but it did seem like the hospital wasn't the best place to end up when you were dedicating your life to fitness.

She'd seen the men coming into the waiting room. One of them had been very agitated, seemingly unaware that blood was streaming out of a bad cut on his forehead. His knuckles were dusted as if he'd done a few rounds and was ready for more, only…bodybuilders weren't boxers. So when the one who wasn't cut told the bleeding guy to wait where he was, and the bleeding guy started hammering into him as if he'd just insulted his mother, she'd been completely taken by surprise and, more concerningly, trapped in a corner.

She saw Rocky appear at the double doors on the opposite site of the waiting room and alongside him was Carter. Carter looked revved up. Ready to take on trouble and show it who was boss. It was two parts sexy to one part scary. There was a wild look in his eye that suggested all his energy was intent on taking down the two men bopping nine shades of testosterone out of one another. Then his eyes met hers and she saw something different altogether. Protection. Care. A silent vow to do whatever he could to make sure she was safe. Now it was two parts sexy and one part scary for a whole other reason. The last thing she wanted was to see him getting hurt.

The nurses and doctors who weren't with patients were busy getting anyone in a wheelchair out of the way. Escorting the elderly to the quiet rooms. Women with children were being hustled into the pediatric waiting room and everyone else was behind the nurse's station or assembling in the minor care triage area. With any luck, someone was calling the orderlies from the psych ward. They were strong and knew how to duck a well-aimed punch. Carter tipped his head and whispered something to Rocky who nodded intently and gave his knuckles a crack. Did they think they could take these two behemoths on? They were insane. Carter was about as strong and sexy as they came, but he wasn't a man mountain, and these two men could throw shade on the Rockies. Carter looked at her then and whatever it was he was lasering at her with those green eyes of his told her she would be okay. He did a quick three count and faster than that had taken, he and Rocky charged the men. A yard or so out, they dove at their ankles. Both men came tumbling down like giants on beanstalks. The floor even shook. One landed in a potted plant and promptly passed out and the other, the bleeding one, crumpled to the floor and began crying, then screaming in a frightening voice, asking why they'd taken all of the ice-cream stands away. He needed ice cream. Now. Chocolate. Vanilla. Strawberry.

The way he was screaming made her never want to eat ice cream again.

All of a sudden it clicked. He had cortico-steroid-induced psychosis. She'd heard about it but had never seen it before. It could cause anything from depression to low sex drive to lethargy to psychosis. This guy was out of control, so she was laying her bets on psychosis. Carter had the guy in a bear hug now and was talking to him in a low steady voice. "We got-cha, buddy. We're here for you. We'll get you all the ice cream you need." He glanced up at Avery. "Heart rate is high, body temp feels elevated, and I'm guessing he's dehydrated." His gaze intensified. "Amongst other things." Clever. He wasn't going to hold a man capable of lifting a refrigerator over his head and offer a public diagnosis of psychosis.

Avery knelt down beside him out of the guy's eyeline and mouthed. "I'm going to get you some injectable hydrocortisone."

Carter nodded and tightened his grip, "You're cool, bud. That's right. Long slow breaths."

She hesitated to move away. It was like watching Iron Man trying to hug it out with the Incredible Hulk when the Hulk could erupt again at any moment. "Do you think you can hold him there?"

"I'll do what I can."

She didn't know why but she had all the confidence in the world he could. She asked one of the nurses behind the counter to get the injection ready and to give her a backup bottle, as well. This guy was big. Real big. She could see his vein throbbing in his neck. His blood pressure was likely up near heart-attack levels.

The orderlies from psych arrived. Rather than give him the injection when he wasn't completely secure, Carter and the three orderlies somehow managed to gently encourage him to climb onto a bed that had secure arm straps. They got the injection into him and, on Carter's instruction, prepared some olanzapine, an antipsychotic medication. Someone who'd responded this badly to an overuse of steroids was going to need a few days in the psych ward to come out of it. She watched as his big old super muscly, scantily clad body was wheeled through the double doors and out of sight.

Avery heard a low groan. She gave one of her own. "Plant pot" guy. He was sitting up, pressing his big meat cleaver of a hand to his head.

"Hi." She ducked her head to catch his gaze. "I'm Avery, can I help you?"

He shook his head. "No, I'm good. That was intense, though."

"Are you sure? Maybe we should give you a quick check."

"Nah, honestly. I think I just need some water and maybe… Could I see him?" He tipped his

head toward the double doors where his mus-
cled-up companion had disappeared.

When Avery's eyes widened in surprise, he
quickly explained, "He's my brother. He keeps
taking steroids even though I tell him that's
some crazy unnatural shit. And today he literally lost it. Was in the middle of a lifting session, then threw the barbell so hard it cracked
the stage floor. If I hadn't tackled him, who
knows what would've happened?"

"How'd you even get him here?"

He shot her an embarrassed smile. "Duct
tape."

Avery tried to keep her expression neutral.

"I cut it off when we got here because I didn't
want you to think I was some sort of psycho."

Fair enough. Arriving as they had had been
interesting enough.

She gave him a proper once-over. This guy
wasn't exactly tiny, but…he was more…lean
rather than inflated. He must be made of pro-
tein shakes.

He shook his head and tipped his forehead
into his hands, remorse catching in his throat.
"I keep telling him he doesn't need to catch
up to me."

"What do you mean?"

"He's my kid brother." He looked up at Avery.
"He was a reedy little thing all through school.

Nerdy. But smart. Helluva lot smarter than me. Sports were always my bag, and not academics, and so I had to punch a few guys out until they knew it wasn't a good idea to shove him in the lockers anymore."

"Sounds like you were protecting him."

He tilted his chin in acknowledgment. "I was, but he hated it. Said he wanted to be able to do the same for me. I said don't be a dumbass. He should be a doctor or lawyer or something that smart folk do. For some stupid reason, he wanted to follow in my footsteps instead of making his own path, and instead of being smarter, he's become stupid. Real stupid."

Avery nodded and tried to give his solid shoulder a squeeze. She failed because of the musculature, but also because there was a ridiculous part of her that was so jealous of him. Having someone to look after. To protect.

Though Carter complained about his sister, she knew his groans of despair came from a place of love. When she'd "won" April as an older sister, she'd followed her around like a lovesick puppy dog as April kept a vigilant eye out for her until she realized she wasn't following anymore. They were walking side by side. Singing as one. Not imagining for one day that either one of them would have to live a life without the other. Losing her had been the most acute way to learn that what they'd shared was one of those precious, precious things that was impossible to replicate without selfless love. It was what Carter had for his sister. What she'd love to do for Carter if things were different.

The thought caught her off guard and pretty much squashed any ability to tell this man that what he was doing was a good thing even if it didn't feel that way. His brother might be a hot mess right now, but he was lucky to have him.

A woman pushed through the double doors and scanned the room. It was Deena Andrews from the admin department. "Quiet in here today."

Avery made a noise that acknowledged the comment, but as her eyes landed on the flyers Deena was about to distribute, her heart lodged too high in her throat to answer.

The Love Conquers Cancer Concert.

With a bright smile, Deena purposefully headed toward one of the notice boards. She tacked up the first flyer and then headed to the next. Avery should've been prepared for this. The calendar worked the same way every year—Christmas, then New Year, then Valentine's Day—but somehow she felt blindsided by the flyer's jolly announcement and, of course, appeal for everyone to give what they could to the Valentine's Day benefit for the oncology ward.

The one she and April used to regularly perform in.

"Looks like fun," said the bodybuilder, then realizing he wasn't going to get an answer from Avery, said something about charity beginning at home and how he'd better knuckle down and find some way to properly help his brother. Get him out of the mess he was in.

If she weren't feeling so out of sorts, she would've tried to think up some advice, but the fistfight topped off by Deena's diligent flyering had loosened something in her. Chipped at the wall she'd built up around her ability to be knocked off her stride. It was all of this talk of siblings. Carter inviting her to meet his sister. This guy, literally and figuratively, torn up over his brother. It made her think of all the variations a sibling relationship could take. Sometimes they kept you safe from bullies. Sometimes they kept you safe from the darker side of yourself. And sometimes they died and took a part of you with them.

All of a sudden, like a dam about to burst inside of her, she began to feel all of the emotions she hadn't been letting herself feel press against her chest wall, demanding more room. More attention. More everything.

She managed to get the forlorn bodybuilding brother some water from the dispenser and put him in touch with one of the registered nurses so that he could see about his brother. Then, knowing she'd used up all of her stores of bravery, she racewalked into the nearest supplies cupboard and dropped to the floor, arms wrapped around her knees, so she could release the howls of pain she'd kept pent-up for so long.

Too soon, someone came in.

"Hey," she heard. "Hey, now."

She was a mess. Shaking, ugly crying, making weird noises that might or might not have been words. And Carter didn't seem to mind at all. He must've grabbed a blanket off one of the shelves, because she felt one being wrapped around her, then his arms followed suit, holding her close, consoling and rocking her, talking in that reassuring drawl of his. He was so solid. So kind. If she could've, she would've disappeared inside of him, but that would be too close to falling in love. And that was the one thing she'd forbidden herself to do when she'd agreed to this harebrained "friends with benefits" thing. They weren't just friends. They were lovers. And she felt like she was free-falling in the sea of emotions that came along with the revelation. If he weren't holding her so close, whispering words of belief that she could survive whatever it was that was tearing her up inside, she could've been lost in it forever. Lost in him. But to her surprise, it was grounding. Eventually, her breath began to steady, her tears abated and she was able to open up her eyes and look into his.

She saw nothing there but kindness. Concern. And at that moment she realized she was far too late in the "don't fall in love" department. She already was.

When Carter pulled his truck into the short drive that led up to Five Acre Farm, he was beginning to have his doubts that his plan was a good one.

The electricity had been on the last time they'd been out here. No porch light today. Could be a blown bulb. He grabbed the pair of grocery store bags from the bench seat of his truck and climbed the porch steps to check it out. Bulb was fine. No electricity.

Damn.

Fuses had probably blown. After filling up the dining room with all the boxes she'd had in storage, they'd asked some workmen he'd heard good things about to come up during the week to start putting the place back together again. Though they hadn't discussed it, they'd both agreed having another team of builders work on the place was best. With a full-time workload, a sister to look after in prison and not much time left…well…he'd rather spend his spare time making love to Avery. He also didn't want her looking at each swoosh of paint and every reinforced wood panel and remember him. If things ended badly between them as they definitely had with his med school ex, he didn't want her to have to hate the house, as well. So, a crew of strangers were doing the work. Ones who left their saw tables and drill packs and piles of tools lying around instead of tidying up each night like he did on a job.

Instead of being mad, he started picking up the mess. He'd promised Avery a beautiful night in her new house and that's what she was going to get. Granted, without electricity, all he had to offer her was a pitch-black, ice-cold house and a mishmash of uncooked ingredients. He checked his watch. She'd insisted upon staying for the rest of her shift, sweet little birdie that she was. His heart ached for her. She hadn't explained why she'd been so upset this afternoon and he hadn't asked, but it was definitely something more than seeing a couple of beefed-up men throw punches at one another. Somehow, he'd known holding her was all she wanted and he was more than happy to do it.

He had an hour and a half before she was

due to arrive. A cooked dinner was out. As was the bubble bath he'd planned to draw for her. He did a quick recalculation and adopted a new plan.

When her headlights finally lit up the living room, his heart started jack hammering against his rib cage as if this were the most important night of his life. It wasn't, but his time with Avery felt precious. Worthy of all his attention. All his heart. And though it freaked him out caring so much—more than he'd planned anyway—he enjoyed giving to someone who wasn't used to receiving. Loved seeing a smile light up her face. Feeling her body lean into his the way it had today when she'd been so upset. He'd liked being her rock. As much as it freaked him out, it had also warmed up corners of his heart he'd thought had long since atrophied. Showed him the heart was resilient. Even his. He gave the place one last scan, hoping like hell she liked what he had done.

He heard her light footsteps upon the porch and then, when she opened the door, he felt the quizzical silence before hearing her slightly confused but comedically singsonged, "Honey! I'm home!"

He walked in from the kitchen, struck dumb by how beautiful she was. The firelight cast her in a warm glow that accentuated the curve of her jawline, the glow of her cheekbones, the fullness of her lips. She'd done her hair into two plaits that hung over her shoulders and something about it made her look both young and womanly all at the same time.

She quirked her chin to the side, her lips twitching as if undecided about whether to smile or frown. "It's freezing outside. Why aren't you wearing a shirt?"

He looked down at himself. He'd been boiling hot fifteen minutes ago. Chopping wood as fast as he could tended to do that. He grinned. "Had to make sure my woman came home to a warm house, didn't I?"

Again, her mouth didn't know what to do with itself. "Is that what I am? Your woman?"

If she hadn't been staring at him, he would've sworn at himself for phrasing it that way. A few weeks ago, he wouldn't have ever referred to a woman as his. If one had asked him that question without prompting, he would've answered it with a solid *no*. But the way Avery had asked it—not possessively, not expectantly—just… curious…it all but turned his guts inside out. Instinctively, he felt the word *yes* form in his mouth. He sure as hell didn't want her to be anyone else's woman. But his brain was rattling through his history of abrupt departures and was telling him to say *no*. Any answer he gave was entering a minefield. He took his first step. "For the next twelve hours, you are all mine."

She let the answer sit between them while she scanned the living room, surprisingly warm from only the heat of the fire. He'd laid out a pile of quilts and some throw pillows he'd found in one of the boxes in the dining room, hoping it'd look cozy. Inviting.

She grinned at him, rubbed her hands together and stretched herself out on the quilt. "Well, I guess I'd better start enjoying it then, shouldn't I?" She tapped the watch she always wore pinned to her scrubs top. "Time's a tickin', cowboy."

He heard her unspoken words loud and clear: *We both know each night could be our last.*

For the first time ever, rather than feel slighted, the shared knowledge of his inevitable departure hurt only because he didn't want to leave. Didn't want to have a day when he wasn't looking forward to seeing her. At work. Here at Five Acre. In bed. The unfamiliar ache filled him like energy, and he set himself a task: to do what she was doing. Making the most of it.

An hour later, he was glad he'd torn around to the local store and hacked up that pile of wood and lit the thirty-odd storm candles he'd found in the cupboard alongside a box of jam jars. Because it turned out, roasting hot dogs in the fireplace with a woman who made him feel more alive than he'd ever felt was pretty much one of the best nights he'd ever had. They'd moved on to dessert—a supersized bag of marshmallows—seeing who had enough patience not to stuff the thing in the flames and set it alight. No surprise there, it was Avery. Despite their fiery first meeting, he saw that she was everything he wasn't. Grounded. Focused on doing her best by her community at the hospital. And determined to put down roots no matter how many people left her behind. Her sister obviously hadn't had a choice. That was a cruel strike of bad fortune. And her grandparents. But her parents… He didn't know how they could've just picked up and left like that. Sold the house she'd grown up in. Left her to fend for herself. Maybe it hadn't been like that. Maybe she'd been invited to come along. To join them in putting as much space between them and the pain they'd endured, the losses they'd suffered. And maybe she'd said no. Maybe she'd needed to feel as much pain as she could endure in order to eventually not feel it anymore.

He considered broaching the topic, but the mood between them was so nice he didn't want to mess it up. So he grabbed his guitar, pulled it out of the case and leaned his back up against the raised stone hearth, closed his eyes and began to play.

It wasn't until he was on his third or fourth song that he realized she'd been singing along. Knew every word to every verse. Maybe she hadn't been singing along at first, maybe she had. But her voice wove itself so perfectly amidst his chords and finger work it felt like it had always been there, waiting for just the right moment to make itself heard.

He opened his eyes. Hers were closed but there were tears pouring out of them, glossing up those cheekbones of hers with sorrow. The words she sang were so full of love and truth he felt his own throat choke up with emotion. She had talent. In spades. When the song came to an end, he didn't start another. She opened her eyes and looked at him. "Why'd you stop playing?"

"Why didn't you tell me you could sing like that?"

"Like what?" She looked genuinely confused.

"Like you just walked onto the stage of the Grand Ole Opry and made the whole damn audience reach for their tissues."

She wiped at her face and looked startled, as if she hadn't realized she'd been crying.

Carter tapped his guitar. "You did know you've been singing along with me, right?"

Her brow furrowed and her hand moved to her throat as if she were checking for some sort of residual sensation. "I guess I was."

She looked as if she didn't know if she were happy or sad about it. She looked at him and their eyes locked together—unspoken words communicating something so powerful he knew Avery Whittacker would always be a part of him no matter what turn fate took.

"I haven't sung a note in almost two years."

"Do you remember what the song was?"

She nodded. "A lullaby."

Goddamn. Singing a lullaby to her dying sister… No wonder she hadn't sung again.

"You must have a magic touch with that guitar of yours," she said, nudging his foot with hers.

He gave a one-shouldered shrug. "I guess it's this cowboy's way of showing he has feelings."

Something that wasn't firelight flared in her eyes.

Before he could register what was happening, she'd moved his guitar out of his lap and replaced it with herself.

CHAPTER ELEVEN

HAVING SEX WITH Carter West was a standout experience at the best of times. Tonight, it was on another level altogether. This, she realized, was what it truly was to make love. He'd seen her frailties and hadn't budged an inch. He'd held her tight, wiped away her tears, made the ramshackle set of walls around them feel like a home and somehow, miraculously, tonight he'd made her sing.

He was half naked already so getting him out of his clothes took half the time. Which was just as well. Because she was *hungry* for him. Judging by the hot kisses he was giving her, kisses that seemed to have no beginning and no hint of an ending, he was feeling the same.

She'd showered at work, but had pulled on some scrubs, and if there was one thing Carter knew how to do, it was how to get her out of her scrubs quick smart. Instead of fast and furious or slow and languorous, tonight was something else completely. Something new. From the moment they became flesh on flesh, their bodies merged like hot molten lava, rocking and moving as if they were one, then two, then one again. Every shift of his body, touch of his lips and caress of his fingertips was mesmeric.

She'd had this big ol' romantic plan to wait. To "christen" the house on the weekend. She'd wanted to make up her new bed—delivery delayed—gussy it up with new cotton bedding—as yet unbought—and for the room to be lit by nothing but starlight. Gray skies were forecast for the next three weeks and the skylight couldn't be installed until April.

But this, here, on the creaking wooden floor in front of a roaring fire filled with logs chopped up by her man—yes, he felt like her man—this was heaven. The house felt like a home, not because of anything the workmen had done or even the nest of quilts and the roaring fire. It felt like home because Carter was in it.

They weren't saying much, but they didn't have to. Singing along with his beautiful guitar playing had uncorked something in her. Opened her up so that there were no secrets anymore. Nothing she wouldn't tell him. Nothing he couldn't tell her. They'd make mistakes and hurt one another, but they'd also care for another. Have each other's backs.

She'd thought she'd been strong these past couple of years. Grief-stricken, sure. But also resilient. Proud. Able to take on new challenges and face them head-on. But what she'd actually been was a shook-up bottle of mixed emotions, no longer able to express herself the way she used to: through music.

The same way April once had, Carter had sensed her mood and played his music soft at first, gentle, then gathering up its pace and emotional punch. April had always made a show of rifling through their songbooks, hemming and hawing over the choices and, as if by magic, picking just the perfect song to lift Avery's spirits or give her that long-awaited cry she might need. She knew when Avery had been upset by a patient dying or happy because they'd gone into remission. She *knew* her. She thought her parents had, too, and though she genuinely didn't resent them for the choice they'd made, she did hope they'd find a way back to one another again. A day when it wouldn't hurt to look at the daughter they still had, a reminder of the one they'd lost.

Being here with Carter, his hands owning her body the way a potter owned clay, she felt cherished. Cared for and appreciated. Desired. It was a potent combination. One that, like it or not, was making its mark. From here on out, everyone would be judged by the "Carter Booth" barometer. And come up short.

The same way her sister had been a rung above everyone else in her life.

But she didn't have her sister anymore and one day she wouldn't have Carter.

Sensing something had changed in her, she felt Carter's hands change their mission. She'd been well on her way to another post-coital orgasm and slightly resented him for stopping what he was doing.

His breath whispered across her lips. "What's going on in that head of yours?"

He was serious. So was she, which was why she didn't want to say anything.

She leaned in to give that juicy lower lip of his a saucy nip, then tried to part them both with her tongue. She encountered resistance. She doubled her efforts. He wasn't playing along. She felt frustrated. Hungry for his touch and, yes, she'd admit it, now that she'd let the earworms in, she also felt scared. Scared of losing this connection she felt. Even considering not feeling his touch at night... It tore at her heart, knowing one day she would have to say goodbye. How was it possible to feel completely whole with someone and know his presence in her life was only temporary?

"You're looking philosophical," he said after pulling back, moving one of his hands so that he could trace curlicues onto her collarbone.

"And you look sexy." She tried to tug his hand back down to where it had been, between her legs, but he kept himself solid. Still.

"I don't want you using me just for my body, hear? I've got two of these." He tapped one of his ears. "They're good for something, too."

She play-snarled at him, but they both heard the bite in it. She was falling in love with Carter Booth and until now hadn't done much to resist it. She thought she had it in her to keep him compartmentalized, but the fact he'd somehow made her sing elicited something else in her. A need to bare herself to him. And she wasn't talking about being naked. She was talking about being an open book. Being that vulnerable was something she hadn't done in a long time. Half of her couldn't imagine living without him. The other half felt like being chest deep in a riptide with the shore getting farther and farther out of reach. She needed to fight to get back to more familiar shores if she was going to survive this.

* * *

"C'mere, you." Carter tucked an arm around her waist and easily turned her so that they were spooning, the both of them facing the fire. He wasn't turning off the conversation. Quite the opposite. He was pulling a halt to their intimacies. Not that there wasn't comfort, or intimacy, in lying in each other's arms without so much as a stitch of clothing between them. There definitely was, but…if they made love again now, they both knew it would be because they were ignoring the elephant in the room. They had feelings for one another and neither of them knew what to do with them.

He pulled her closer when she began to tremble. "I've got you," he said.

"For how long?"

He wanted to say *forever*. With every pore in his body, he did, but they both knew it would be a lie. He wanted to assure her that they'd get over one another soon enough. That what they were experiencing was that crazy endorphin-fueled rush of lust that made any new couple think they couldn't live without the other, but that would've been a lie, too.

"As long as I'm able."

She whipped around, propped her head on her hand and, eyes blazing, asked, "What exactly am I meant to do with that?"

"We knew this might happen."

"We knew we'd have hot sex," she parried.

Good point. But… "No. We knew there was something more between us than lust."

She harrumphed. He mimicked the sound and, as he'd hoped, a smile flickered across her face. She gave his chest a poke with her finger. Then, with less aggravation, began tracing little designs onto his chest while she thought.

"Why'd you invite me to come see your sister?"

Normally, this was the part where he'd say he wanted her to see what she was up against. Witness, firsthand, the reason why his heart would never be fully open to a relationship. Then the girl would back out, accept that things had come to a natural conclusion and go on to find another relationship.

Cassidy could be vile and though she openly resented Carter's "interference" in her life, she was contrarily embittered toward anyone else who took his time. His affections. So, yeah, if Avery were anyone else, he would've said five minutes with Cassidy was all she'd need to tamp down anything approaching actual feelings for him.

But she wasn't anyone else. She would come to the prison with him, no doubt charm the socks off Cassidy and then he'd be on brand new terrain he wouldn't know what to do with.

All of which had to mean something, didn't it? It suggested that they weren't just good at having sex. They were good at being together.

From the moment he'd laid eyes on her, Avery had somehow become a part of him. The same way the knee bone was connected to the thighbone, Avery Whittacker was connected to his heart. And it wouldn't tear when the time to say goodbye finally hurtled toward them—it would break.

She was still waiting for an answer and he owed it to her to be honest. "I guess when I said we'd be friends with benefits, I hadn't realized the *friends* part of it would come to mean so much."

He cleared his throat and stared past her at the fire. It went beyond that and he knew it, but if he declared his real feelings for her, he might as well pull the plug on the whole thing right now. He couldn't tell her he was in love with her. Because then he wouldn't just be walking away from her, he'd be walking away from the man he was when he was with her—the one he'd wanted to become all these years.

"Is there anything we can bring her?" Avery asked.

He shook his head. "Not unless you've got a change jar that you can raid. We can get her treats from the vending machine." He snorted out a laugh. "I've never met a woman who likes cheesy puffs more than my sister."

Avery grinned that open, happy smile of hers. "Cheesy puffs?"

"Yes, ma'am. There isn't a food additive or artificial flavoring that doesn't have my sister's name on it."

Avery pressed her hand to his heart. "It must take its toll on you."

"Her awful eating habits?" He huffed out another humorless laugh. He knew what she meant—watching his sister systematically destroy herself. "If you don't want to come, I understand. After what you've been through—"

"After what I've been through, I should be stronger than I am," she said, her voice hot with feeling.

Enough to pull his eyes back to hers. "What do you mean?"

She kept her hand solidly on his chest, his heartbeats pressing themselves against her palm as if it were a salve. And maybe it was. Maybe love was that simple.

"Do you know why I was crying in that supplies cupboard earlier today?"

He shook his head no, but he had a rough idea.

"After the ruckus with the weight-lifting guys, Deena came in from Admin."

His radar shot up. "Did she say something to upset you?"

"No. She put up some notices." Her lips twitched as she fought a private battle for composure. "For the Valentine's Day benefit."

"I've seen those. They're putting them up like wallpaper around the hospital. I don't really recognize any of the performers."

Avery looked back at him. "You would've two years ago, and the five years preceding."

"You sang?" He gave her shoulder a squeeze. "I bet everybody loved that."

"They did. They loved both of us."

And then he got it. The singing teacher. The house. The posters. Him pulling out his guitar and unwittingly reminding her of the woman she used to be. The one she could never be again.

"So, I take it they didn't approach you."

"They did and I said no! How could I even have considered saying no when I know first-hand just how much a top-rate cancer center means to people? It's not just money for research. It's support for families, for the hospice. Everything. And I was too wrapped up in myself to help." She reached out and tugged a blanket to her, wrapped it around her shoulders and sat up. He followed suit.

"I think people would understand." He meant

the words to comfort, but they only seemed to lance her with more pain.

"But if I were a truly good person, the person April thought I was, I should never ever, no matter what I'm going through, want anyone else to endure a similar amount of pain."

"I don't follow."

"This may sound like humble bragging, but it isn't meant to."

He nodded for her to go on.

"When April and I were on the roster, a lot of people came to the benefits. A *lot*."

"Okay." He wasn't sure where this was heading.

"Including a few bigwigs from the record labels."

"You're going to have to spell this out for me darlin'. I'm about as 'show biz' naive as they come."

She pointed her hands toward herself. "They wanted us."

"For a record?"

He whistled. "If your sister could sing anything like you can, I'm not surprised by that."

Avery's expression turned grim. "She could. And play the guitar. But then she got sick."

Ah. The Lord giveth. Then the Lord taketh away.

"So did they approach you again?"

She nodded. "I said no way. I couldn't do it without my sister."

He didn't mention the fact they were sitting in the house her sister was also meant to be living in.

"I know!" She put her hands up. "You're wondering how I could buy this house without her but say no to a record deal?"

He made a big check in the space between them. "You can tick mind reading off your list anyway."

She smiled, then wilted beneath her blanket. "It's just... I was watching that guy take all his brother's punches and then reminded myself how you have forsaken any kind of permanence in your life to catch your sister every time she falls and all of a sudden it hit me. Even though it's hard, and sometimes physically painful, you're both still doing everything you can for your siblings and I'm not. I let the one thing I know in my heart April would've wanted me to do on her behalf fall to the wayside."

"Become a country star?"

"No. Help people."

"What are you talking about?" He gave one of her plaits a little tug. "You help people. Every day at work."

"I know, but I mean above and beyond. We did that concert every year without thinking because it was that one step further. We also used to volunteer at a soup kitchen once a month. We knew it wouldn't cure homelessness same as we knew singing wouldn't cure cancer, but they definitely helped inch things along." She lowered her voice to something deep and gravelly. "'Some progress is better than none.'" Her smile was soft and faraway. "It was something my Pawpaw used to say when we were training horses and really, life's no different, is it?"

Carter shook his head. No. Life wasn't much different.

Avery was on a roll now, thank goodness, because he was a bit too wrong-footed by the comment to hold the X-ray up to his own life, the decisions he'd made, wondering if what he was doing right now was progress or sheer stupidity. Hobbling himself and his sister? Or helping? There was no easy answer.

"As long as you're going forward..." Avery put her fingers to her eyes, then pointed them out, "...looking forward, it's an improvement. And doing that concert was the first thing I backed away from after she died because it was too acute a reminder of what had been taken from me. It felt personal and I should've realized it wasn't personal. It's just life. It can kick your knees out from under you and what you have to do is get back up again, no matter how much it hurts. I've been sitting on the ground, Carter. Just sitting, waiting for life to happen to me."

"I wouldn't call riding a mechanical bull on New Year's Eve to get the deposit money for the house of your dreams sitting idle."

She tipped her head back and forth. "It wasn't exactly helping society, though, was it?"

Carter had an idea, then backed away from it.

"What?" She poked his knee with her finger through her blanket.

He grinned and gave her cheek a stroke with the back of his hand. "You mind reading again?"

"Trying to, but I think you're going to have to help me."

"I was wondering…" He tipped his head and met her expectant gaze. "What if I were to offer to play alongside you? I won't sing. No one would appreciate that for an offer, but I'd play for you."

She blew out a long slow breath, but her eyes didn't leave his.

"Right up there on stage? In front of hundreds of strangers? You'd do that?"

He nodded. He'd do it naked and upside down if it lit up her eyes like they were now. "Sure would. Any songs you like unless they're heavy metal and then you'd have to find yourself someone who has plugs in their guitar."

She smiled. "I wouldn't want anyone else."

"Is that your version of a yes?"

She nodded, then shook her head no. "It's a can I think about it?"

"Absolutely. Now." He pulled her close to him and dropped a kiss onto her forehead, then just as gently onto her lips. "Maybe we should blow out these candles and get some shut-eye?"

Holding her in his arms that night felt sweeter than any other had. If she went for it, he knew it would be a step in the right direction for her. Only question was could he be brave enough to do the same in his own life?

CHAPTER TWELVE

"THREE BAGS! CARTER, you're spoiling me. What a perfect big brother you are."

Carter rolled his eyes. Cassidy was putting on one heck of a show. Only thing was he couldn't tell if it was a thriller or a chick flick. She seemed to like Avery, but Cassidy seemed to like everyone at first. Before she pulled the knives out. Figuratively, of course. The most lethal weapon she was allowed here at prison was her paper-thin mattress and, surprise, surprise, they didn't let them haul those into the visiting room.

On the flipside, Avery was on top form. Not over the top, not clinging onto him, not overly brightly attentive to his sister. Just a friend along for the ride. A story Cassidy wasn't buying.

"So, what brings you to this neck of the woods?" Cassidy's question was directed solely toward Avery. "Drawn by the catering?" Cassidy held out a half-eaten bag of cheesy puffs.

Carter tipped his head into his hands. Why the hell he'd thought this was a good idea was beyond him.

To his surprise, Avery took a few and had a munch. She frowned at the couple remaining in her hand.

"What's wrong? Not to your liking? I hear the caviar ones are due in on Tuesday, if they're more your style."

She was testing Avery and both women knew it.

"Nah, I'm good. I'm just trying to figure out if I like the crunchy ones with hot sauce more than the puffy ones." She jammed her two remaining puffs between her upper lip and her teeth, then gave them both a good gawk at her orange fangs. They all laughed, and Avery ate her "fangs," pronouncing them delicious. Cassidy's hackles went down, and her body language changed from defensive to genuinely inquisitive. Her eyes pinged between the two of them as if they were divining rods of truth. Before he could think of some way to steer the conversation away from the inevitable, his kid sister pounced. "What's going on with you two anyway?"

Carter said, "We're colleagues," at the same time as Avery said, "We're friends."

Damn. He'd screwed that one up. Rather than

bristle, Avery shot him a look that said, *It's cool. I know this is weird.*

"'Outside of work' friends?" Cassidy pushed.

He and Avery shared a look. Cassidy burst into laughter. "Don't even try to lie. I know a pair of 'loved up' people when I see them." She sighed. A wistful look wrapped itself around her so tight Carter felt his own heart constrict.

"You know you're my number one girl, Cass."

Cassidy frowned at him. Avery's expression stayed static.

"You're allowed to have girlfriends, Carter."

As two pairs of eyes lit on him, all the breath in his body felt like it had been hit by liquid nitrogen.

Here it was. The rock and the hard place. Cassidy knew damn straight why he didn't do relationships. Because the one that mattered most was family.

He felt Avery's thigh brush against his. His instinct was to reach out and grab her hand, but what signal would that send?

The wrong one.

It was like swallowing razor blades, knowing he couldn't give her what she deserved. Hell. What they both deserved. A family of their own.

Knowing there was no right answer, Carter

cleared his throat and tried to shift on his stool—the kind that was welded to the table so you couldn't throw it anywhere.

"Do you share a space with someone nice?" Avery asked.

Clever woman. Easing the tension but still staying real. He didn't know what he'd done to deserve her, but at this precise moment Avery felt heaven-sent. Little wonder she'd slid under his skin so easily. He just couldn't wrap his head around why she'd let him slide under hers. An inevitable goodbye didn't seem the best prospect for a romantic partner. It was little consolation, but at least she knew what was coming. With her sister, she hadn't. Maybe losing her sister had made her into the type of person who flipped ahead to the last page of a book before letting herself get past chapter one.

Cassidy shrugged. "She's all right. A bit of a joiner."

"How do you mean?"

"She's always dragging me along to the group activities."

Carter nodded. That was new. And from the way she was avoiding eye contact, he wasn't entirely convinced there was much *dragging* involved. Had something changed during his sister's stint in solitary?

Avery asked something he hadn't caught, and

Cassidy was shaking her head. "I don't know which is worse. Solitary confinement or the group activities."

"What ones do they have you doing?" he asked.

She glared at him. "They're voluntary, but I've been going to the—" She hesitated, flicked her eyes at Avery, then told her instead of him. "I've been going to the AA meetings. They're in the chapel." She quickly covered with an explanation. "It's the nicest room in the whole place, so…"

"Cool," Avery said without judgment. "Do they have a choir?"

Cassidy hooted. "No one in their right mind would want to hear me sing." She was about to reach across to Carter, then glanced at the guard and pulled her hands back into her lap. "Has Carter sung to you?"

"Not a note." Avery surreptitiously gave his leg a squeeze. She'd caught that Carter was feeling the sting of not being able to hold his sister's hands in his. In prison, it was a chance to pass contraband. In real life, it was a way to say I love you without saying anything.

This was the first time he'd had someone witness his pain firsthand, then offer him comfort for it. Avery's gesture dislodged something in his chest he couldn't quite put a name to.

Cassidy ran a few croaky notes past them. "Let that be a warning to you. Booths don't sing."

"What do they do?" Avery asked.

Cassidy shrugged, and in the blink of an eye, he watched his sister retreat inside herself to an extent that scared him. Sometimes he thought he knew her better than anyone. Other times he felt like he didn't know her at all. This was one of those times. He ached to know where she went when she disappeared like this.

"How're you feeling these days?" he asked, then from the sharp look on her face, wished he hadn't.

"Peachy," came the terse reply. She stood up and brushed a few crumbs off her blue top. "I think they're about to call time. I'd better get going."

All three of them knew it was a lie. They'd been here maybe ten minutes, max. She got four hours of visiting time a month, which he spread out into eight half-hour visits. Rather than push it, he decided to talk with the warden, see if they'd tack the time onto his next visit. She looked tired. Probably wasn't eating enough if the loose fit of her uniform was anything to go by. She was the polar opposite of Avery—a woman very obviously in the prime of her life, her cheeks still glowing from this morning's run and the shower they might've accidentally on purpose taken together.

He thought bringing Avery here would be... Hell. He didn't know what.

Maybe it was an act of self-sabotage. The only way he could show Avery what a mess his sister was and, by extension, him. Or maybe he wanted to show his sister that life didn't have to be lived the way she was doing it. After all, Avery had experienced some incredibly hard knocks in life, but she seemed determined to get back up again. Cassidy? Not so much.

He didn't know anymore. The only thing that seemed to be coming out of this was the fact that sitting with the two halves of his life made him feel more torn apart than whole. Not the goal at all.

Once they were back in his truck, waiting for the engine to warm up, Avery asked, "You all right?"

The engine choked. He cranked the key again. Too hard. He needed a new truck.

Who was he kidding? He needed a new life. The one he'd been struggling to maintain clearly wasn't working.

He made a noise that might've passed for yes.

"Can't be easy," she said, giving his hand a squeeze as he grabbed ahold of the gear lever and jammed it into Reverse.

He didn't want her pity and she wasn't giving it. Just acknowledging one of those so-called "universal truths." Seeing a sibling locked up made you sad. End of story.

She shifted around so she was facing him. "Want to do something that'll put that Stetson of yours to work?"

Yeah. He did. Anything to take his mind off this disaster of a visit. He put the truck into gear and made a silent promise to pop in on his own tomorrow. See if he could sweet-talk the warden into letting him take a look at their medical facilities.

"What's this plan of yours, then?"

Avery couldn't have wiped the smile off her face if she'd tried. Carter on a horse was like ice cream and chocolate sauce. Biscuits and gravy. Poetry in motion was another way to put it. He and the steed the stable manager had chosen for him—a gorgeous chestnut stallion called Fair-weather—were whipping around those barrels as if they'd been doing it for years.

He pulled up to her and grinned. The dullness she'd seen in his eyes after their visit to the prison was now replaced by bright happy sparks of adrenaline and achievement. A bit like he looked after he'd come out of an intense surgery or fresh from delivering someone good news after a potentially life-altering scan. While it was good to have this version of Carter back in the room—or barn in this case—she knew it wasn't a replacement for talking about how things had gone with his sister.

"You think you can beat that time?" he asked.

They both glanced up at the clock.

She fuzzed out a raspberry. "Easy."

He made a noise that acknowledged the fighting talk and then another one that suggested he kinda liked the look of her on a horse as much as she liked the look of him on one. "Well, go on, then."

She tapped her heels into her horse's sides and set off the way she intended to finish, at high speed. When she got back, he had his hat off, pressed over his heart and was blowing out that same low sexy whistle he'd sounded the first night she met him. And just like that night, he took her breath away. Same as he had every day since. It was almost impossible to believe that this man was a stranger a few weeks ago. Now, she felt like she knew him almost as well as she knew herself. She knew his ribs were extra ticklish. And that sliding her hand along the inside musculature of his thigh made him groan. Same as kisses on his throat. She knew when he'd made a diagnosis for a patient and that it wasn't good by the way he pulled up a stool and took their hands in his. She could tell when he'd lost a patient by the tension in his shoulders. And she knew he had feelings for her but that he didn't know what to do with them.

Snap, Carter Booth. Snap.

She'd always wondered what it would feel like to look at a man and think, *My goodness, he's all mine.* She allowed herself 99 percent possession for just this moment, knowing deep down he'd never be wholly hers. Especially now she'd met his sister. Blood did run deep. And in their case, it was "Grand Canyon" deep.

Carter squinted at the timer, then pulled his horse around to the starting line. Her eyes dropped to enjoy the sight of his legs making the most of his blue jeans as he stretched out, using the stirrups as a ballast. Sex god, loving brother and a man who heard the call of medicine as loud and clear as she did. How on earth was she going to let him go? Even thinking about it felt like being wrenched in two. It took her a couple of seconds to realize he was speaking to her.

"You okay?" He looked concerned.

"Fine."

He narrowed his eyes as if he didn't believe her but made a tactical choice not to comment on it. He tightened his grip on the reins. "I'm thinking about going around again."

She forced herself to laugh, hoping it masked the aching feeling that got knocked open inside her whenever she thought about saying goodbye. "Don't tell me you mind being beaten by a girl."

"Oh, I don't," he said, steadying his horse with a big old hand along the chestnut's neck. "Especially when she is all woman." And then he took off.

She reminded herself it was a view she was going to have to familiarize herself with. The backside of him. He'd spelled it out for her before, but now that she'd seen him with Cassidy, it made his promise that he'd be leaving all too real. And who was she to fault him for doing everything he could for his sister?

He was brother and father to her. Doctor. Protector. Everything and everyone a sickly child needed when their parents didn't or couldn't shoulder the load themselves.

She knew that she'd let herself fall too deeply in love with him. Her heart was his for crushing or, more to the point, abandoning when the time came.

He rode back in, his face alight with undiluted joy and flashed her a full wattage smile. If she hadn't begun to let the crystals of fear chill the edges of her heart, it would've melted her into a molten puddle of, *Yes, please, cowboy.*

"Let's go out," he said later when they were racking up their saddles.

"What? For something to eat?"

"No." His eyes were still lit up the way they'd been when he'd managed to tease a few seconds off his time and tie with her. "Let's go dancing."

She looked down at her horsey jeans and thick layering of tops. "Err…"

He pulled her into his arms, nestled into the crook of her neck and whispered, "You look absolutely perfect." He pulled back and warmed her from tip to toe with that perfect grin of his. "Let's go line dancing."

Carter knew it was idiotic. Clinging to a fantasy like this. But holding Avery in his arms, feeling her body respond to his as they both let the music pour through them—it was pure magic. He was as certain as the boots on his feet that he'd never find a woman like this again. It was the first time in his life he wished his sister would actually serve her full sentence. But what, then? Three years down the line, leaving Avery would be next to impossible.

He let a thought creep in that he rarely gave air to. What if he didn't? What if he stayed.

"Penny for 'em?" Avery pulled back and did a little twirl into his arms.

He smiled down at her and pulled her in tight. Intuitive woman. He tipped his head toward the stage where the band was playing. "I was wondering what it would be like to hear you sing up there. See couples swaying like this to the sound of your beautiful voice." It wasn't a total lie. The sound of her voice weaving in and out of his guitar strings ranked up there in the "special moments" department. And his list was short.

She looked up at the stage, then back at him and something deep in his gut told him she was feeling the same kind of sentimental. As if they were practicing their goodbyes so that when the time actually came, it wouldn't hurt as much.

"It's not an open mic night," she said. "If it was…"

His heart crashed against his rib cage. There was a bright light shining in those dark eyes of hers that told him she'd do it if he could make it happen.

Before she could come up with an excuse not to sing, he was walking the two of them off the sawdust-covered dance floor to the bar. He got her a drink then while he was waiting for his and had a quiet word with the barman. He knew this window of opportunity could close real quick. When the band finished their song, the bearded owner went up, had a word and the singer smiled in understanding.

"Ladies and gentlemen, we've got a special treat for you. We've been told this woman is an angel by day at St. Dolly's Hospital and has a voice to match. Everyone, please give up some cheers for Nashville's own Avery Whittacker."

Carter didn't mind one bit when Avery punched him in the arm for the OTT intro because her cheeks were glowing, her smile was hitting each ear and, most importantly, she was walking up onto that stage. He switched out with the guitar player and once she whispered a song title to him, he let her voice guide him straight to heaven. Because he hadn't been lying when he'd described her voice and by the sound of the audience's appreciative feedback, they didn't think so, either. She'd chosen a love song, which he hadn't really taken in until he realized she was singing it to him, for him, about him. Because it was country music, it naturally involved a healthy serving of heartache, but the overall message was clear. Avery Whittacker loved him. Faults and all. And in that moment, he felt complete.

CHAPTER THIRTEEN

"You look like a happy bunny today." Valentina gave her a hip bump as she entered the nurses' station.

"Do I?" Avery lifted up her tablet and pretended it was a mirror.

Avery was struggling to know if she was floating on clouds or waiting for the ground to fall out from under her. She hadn't exactly told Carter she'd loved him those few nights back when they'd played together at the Cattleman's Bar & Grille, but she knew by the way he'd made love to her that night and every night since that he'd got the message. Between that and the piles of sawdust he'd racked up between shifts, helping her turn her house from an eyesore into something beautiful, she knew that, in his own way, he loved her, too. It hurt, though. Waiting for the inevitable. So, despite all of the happy feels, they were all twisted up with the same sort of pain she'd felt when her sister had received her diagnosis.

"I told you I don't want to be seen by a doctor!"

Avery whipped around toward the sliding entryway. She knew that voice. It was her singing teacher, Bonnie. Her "boy toy," Levi, was pushing her in on a wheeled office chair, and from the looks of things, Levi had tied her to it.

Avery did a quick mental whip through of vitals she should be observing. Bonnie's level of consciousness was certainly fine. Her face was red with rage, indignation, high blood pressure or a heady combination of all three. But the fact she wasn't strictly fighting being in the chair made Avery wonder if there was a part of Bonnie that was grateful her boyfriend had gone to extreme measures to get her here.

Avery ran up to them along with Dr. Chang and Carter.

Dr. Chang set about undoing the ropes and giving Levi what for. "We don't restrain patients to bring them in."

"Oh, yeah?" Levi shot back. "What if the woman you love doesn't have enough energy in her legs to shop for an engagement ring?"

Avery's eyes shot to Bonnie's. Bonnie pursed her lips. They both looked at her ring finger on her left hand. It was empty. "I just didn't want to go through the embarrassment of having none of them fit. I'm starting a diet this afternoon." She whipped a finger in Levi's direction, "Not that I'm agreeing to marry you. Not after this!"

"Hush, woman. You know you love me." Levi clucked, shifting a few of Bonnie's big glossy curls back over her shoulder. "And I love her, too. Even if she is an ornery old mule."

"I am not old!" Bonnie protested. "Honestly. How could anyone marry a man who described them as old?"

Avery took one of Bonnie's hands in her own. Her fingers were plump. Always had been. But today they were cold, pale and a bit swollen. She glanced down. As usual, Bonnie was wearing a long skirt, so it was tricky to see her legs, but Avery would've bet money that they were swollen. Painfully so. Avery could hear a slight wheeze whenever Bonnie drew a breath. Pulmonary hypertension? High blood pressure in the lung's blood vessels could be making her heart work twice as hard, which could lead to long-term damage. Levi had been right to bring her in.

Avery tried to casually check Bonnie's pulse point to see what was going on, but Bonnie was clearly no stranger to surreptitious medical care.

"No, you don't, young lady. You do not have my permission."

Avery held up her hands. "Okay. Fine. We'll do it your way."

"My way is over a stack of pancakes down at the Waffle House, which is where I thought we were going. So unless you're planning on joining me, I guess we'd better say our farewells."

Out of the corner of her eye, Avery could see that Carter had magicked up a proper wheelchair and left it beside her, before turning his attention to Levi who was more than willing to offer up Bonnie's list of symptoms. As Avery tried to extract what information she could from a reluctant Bonnie, she suddenly saw Carter half carry, half guide Levi into the wheelchair Bonnie was refusing to get into.

"It's my arm, not my heart!" Levi protested. But his hand was clutching his chest and it was easy enough to see Levi was either having a massive angina attack or a heart attack.

"Coming through!" Carter took hold of Levi's wheelchair and steered him through to the acute care section of the emergency room. Bonnie was doing her best to follow but was struggling. Knowing Levi would receive the best possible care from Carter, Avery took ahold of her arm and steered Bonnie to a row of chairs outside the curtained-off area they had swept Levi into.

"I want to be in there!"

"I know you do, Bonnie, but there's no room."

"Tell me every single thing they're doing to him. I love you, baby! Levi! You hear me! I love you!" Bonnie shouted through the curtain, then as much as her ample frame would allow, she turned on Avery. "If I can't be there, you explain to me what's happening. He's my man and this is my fault!" Avery knew protesting at a moment like this was time wasted, so she stared at the curtain and began to talk. She'd actually seen Carter deal with this exact situation a fair few times, so she could picture his calm, exacting movements with ease. "He'll have Levi's shirt open and will be attaching electrodes to his chest and limbs."

"What for?"

"It's an ECG. An electrocardiogram. He'll be given thrombolytics."

"Speak plain to me, honey! I don't talk doctor."

"We call them clot busters—they help dissolve any blood clots that might be blocking blood flow to Levi's heart. The sooner he receives them, the less likely it is he'll have heart damage."

"So it's actually a blessing he brought me here?"

"Very much so."

Avery took Bonnie's hands in hers. "He'll probably be giving some nitroglycerin to help with the chest pain. It can also improve blood flow to the heart."

"He's got a huge heart. Huge! I love you, baby!"

A weak, "I love you, too, you old mule!" came through the curtain.

Bonnie pursed her lips and glared at Avery. "I'm guessing that's a sign he'll live?"

Nothing was certain in life, but she knew Carter and his team would do their best. "It's a good sign. He'll need some tests to see what's actually going on. They'll take blood samples and probably get him to have some scans. He may need a coronary angioplasty and stenting."

Bonnie gasped. "That sounds serious."

"They are, but they could also save his life."

"They aren't going to put those shocker things on him, are they?"

"Not unless he has a cardiac arrest."

"What's that?"

"When the heart beats irregularly or stops altogether."

Bonnie paled. "No. No, no, no. Levi's got far too much life in him for that to happen." She

raised her voice. "And we still got us a wedding to plan, you hear?"

Through the curtain, Avery could hear
Carter and his team murmuring soft instruc-
tions back and forth, low enough that Levi's
response came through loud and clear. "Only
if you agree to see that vascular doctor your
little friend there told you to see *weeks* ago!"

Bonnie sat back in her chair with a huff. It
was easy to see she knew he was right, but the
decision still had to be hers.

Avery kept her voice neutral. "Can we take
that as a yes?"

Bonnie pushed herself up to standing, took a
step toward the curtained area where they were
treating Levi, then whirled around. She went
a bit unsteady, so Avery leaped up to give her
some balance. It looked as though she'd gone
into some sort of trance, but realized Bonnie
was actually staring at one of the posters for
the Valentine's Day benefit.

Her eyes shifted to Avery's. "That's the concert you and your sister used to do."

"Sure is." Avery looked away, practically
hearing the wheels in Bonnie's head turning.
The curtain around Levi's acute care bed was
whipped open by Valentina. Carter was at the
head of the bed and a weak but smiling Levi
lit up when he saw Bonnie, cheeks instantly

streaking with tears. "See what lengths I'll go to get you to marry me?"

Bonnie grabbed his hand and walked along his gurney as best she could, but it was easy to see that their usual pace was too much for her. Levi asked them to stop for a minute. "So I can talk with my beloved."

"Don't you go dying on me," Bonnie scolded.

"I think I could say the same to you, my beautiful young woman."

Bonnie softened at his description. She held Levi's hand in hers, careful not to knock the needle taped into his hand delivering blood-thinning medication. "I mean it. You can't die."

"So do I," said Levi. "Now give me a kiss because the sooner I take these tests, the sooner I can get out of here and bring you to your doctor's appointment so we can go ring shopping."

Bonnie gently pressed a kiss onto his pale cheek and waved goodbye long after he'd disappeared into the imaging department. When she finally dropped her arm, she took both of Avery's hands in hers, a very serious expression on her face. "I will go see that doctor friend of yours. What was her name again?"

"Dr. Iliana Costa. She's great at what she does and if there's a problem, she'll do her level best to help you solve it." Avery pictured drawing a music note onto Bonnie's wrist for Lia, so she'd know Bonnie was one of hers.

Bonnie gave her hands a squeeze and repeated, "I will go…on one condition."

Avery nodded, expecting it to be something about keeping an eye on Levi who would, no doubt, need to spend the night for observation or, depending upon what the scans said, have an operation. "Okay."

"You promise?"

Avery laughed. "So long as it's not committing a crime, I'm in."

Bonnie gave a satisfied nod, then said, "I'd like to see you sing at the concert. For your sister. She'd want you up there, shining like the star you are."

Everything around Avery slowed down. She could hear the *ba-boom* of her heartbeat. The white noise of blood rushing to her brain. The slow-motion slideshow of that awful, awful day when they'd lowered the casket containing her sister's body into the ground, her mother's keening drowning out everything around them. And then, to her surprise, the muscle memory of how she felt when she sang with her sister returned. The warmth she felt in her heart, the smile she could never quite wipe from her face, the love radiating from the center of her truest self. It was a feeling she'd felt recently. Giving voice to her emotions, the only way she knew how. Through music.

To her complete shock, she said yes, then quickly amended. "There's someone I'd like to accompany me."

Bonnie gave a sly grin. "That handsome doctor who just saved my Levi?"

Avery blushed. "How'd you know?"

"I'm fat, not blind!"

Avery didn't contain her grin at being seen. "Shall we pinkie promise on this? That you'll see Lia in exchange for one charity gala?"

Bonnie lifted her pinkie into the space between them. "I thought you'd never ask."

Avery stopped jumping up and down long enough to ask, "Are you sure?"

"With every fiber in my body." Carter started ticking off his fingers. "Hearing you sing. Helping out the hospital. Having a date on Valentine's Day… What's not to love?"

She stared at him for a couple of seconds, started rapid blinking, then said, "Well, then. I guess I'd better go put a set together."

He watched her go and wondered what all that was about, but then realized he'd just walked through a perfect opportunity to tell her that he loved her…and hadn't.

They spent the next week in a happy haze.

Working at the hospital and building a beautiful set of songs he knew would get people draining their bank accounts. Avery was a wonder and it felt good to be part of something that was bigger than himself. That would be giving back to the industry that had kept him whole while the rest of his life floundered.

Just a few days shy of the Valentine's benefit, he could feel the excitement rising like spring sap in Avery. Everything she did had an added zip to it. Bandaging patients came with some cheerful artwork. She hummed while she took vitals. Even signing patients out elicited a playful curtsy or a jaunty cowgirl salute. He liked seeing her this way and was enjoying basking in her glow.

He had just finished booting up a poor guy who'd ruptured his Achilles tendon during an ill-advised game of squash when he heard calls for help from the secure care department. He took off at a run, shooting a quick smile to Avery when she appeared beside him.

The doors to the ambulance bay swung open and the paramedics wheeled in a gurney with a slight figure cocooned in a blanket on it. The patient's hair was dark, making her slightly jaundiced skin seem even more so.

Cassidy.

As he fought to keep his hammering heart

under control, Stacy, the paramedic, was rattling off the facts. "Female inmate known to suffer from sickle cell anemia found collapsed in her cell after exercise session at local penitentiary. Hydroxyurea administered on site along with liquid ibuprofen and oxygen. Morphine denied."

Carter ground his teeth together. He'd bet any amount of money they'd denied her morphine because they thought she was faking it. It was a problem in prison hospitals. Inmates faking symptoms. Prison doctors doubting patient's believability. He knew his sister's pride would've had her lying throughout the entire Brief Pain Inventory, the barometer they used for monitoring effective treatment of pain. Only trouble was pain was the main barometer of sickle cell. If you were feeling it, you needed treatment. Immediately. So no wonder she looked like hell.

"Carter." He felt a hand on his arm. Avery. "You need to sit this one out."

"Like hell I do."

Avery flinched at the bite in his tone. He was too upset to fix it. He did what he always did—grabbed ahold of one side of the gurney and said, "Follow my lead. She's my sister. I know what to do." He started rattling off her blood type, her history, the last time she'd had an SCD crisis. He'd made himself a specialist on the topic, stopping short of doing it full time because he knew the ER would always be her first port of call. His sister had never been one to come in on a suspicion that things weren't going well. She always waited until those sickle cells traveled through her tiny blood vessels, got stuck and clogged the blood flow.

"Booth!" Dr. Chang somehow inserted herself between Carter and the gurney. "I don't know what sort of hospitals you've worked in before, but this one recognizes that you have a conflict of interest. Step aside."

Avery mouthed, *We've got this.*

He wanted to feel assured. His brain knew Avery was right. She and the rest of the team were completely capable, if not better qualified to look after his sister than he was right now. He'd been wrong to try to use his rank and his emotions to overpower Avery. He just got so twisted up inside because each time Cassidy was sick like this, it brought him those few steps closer to being the only Booth left standing.

He watched, helplessly, as they wheeled her into the secure unit and began calling for blood transfusions and hooking her up to all the necessary monitors. And then something kicked back into place he'd almost forgotten about. He wasn't the guy who stood by and watched other people look after his sister. He was the guy who had promised to protect as best he could.

He yanked back the curtain and began barking out orders over Dr. Chang's. Cassidy was in a bad state. Worse than he'd seen her in years. She might have splenic sequestration. If she'd been found passed out, those damn cells of hers had had more than enough time to get trapped in the spleen and cause an enlargement. Beneath the oxygen mask they'd rigged up on her, he could see her lips were pale and that her breathing was coming in quick, short bursts. When Dr. Chang palpated her left side, she flinched. Unsurprisingly, the heart monitor was up in the higher altitudes, precisely where it shouldn't be.

Just as he was demanding she be brought in for a scan to see if she needed a splenectomy, he felt two sets of hands clamp onto his arms and the security guys were frog marching him backward out of the treatment room. The door was shut in his face.

He broke free and pounded his fist against the bulletproof glass window. Couldn't they see Cassidy needed him? *They* needed him. His insight. His point-by-point history of her condition. His photographic memory of her medicines, her frailties, her strengths and the way they could make the most of them. His eyes met Avery's. Seeing the depth of concern in those dark brown eyes of hers should've had a soothing effect. But this time it didn't because for the first time since they'd met, he saw, clear as day, that he'd been an idiot to start something he couldn't finish.

Watching Avery's concern turn to sorrow felt like being slammed in the chest with a pickax.

So he started hollering through the window about how he hoped they were checking for leg ulcers and strokes and deep vein thrombosis. Pulmonary embolisms. Increased blood coagulation. All things he knew they knew, but shouting was better than sitting around doing nothing.

The charge nurse ran up to him and touched his arm. He whipped around and shouted, "What?"

When he saw fear in her eyes, he knew he'd gone too far. Way too far.

Barely above a whisper, she said there was a little boy who'd suffered a compound fracture after falling off his pony. He gave himself one hell of a shake and forced himself back into the land of common sense. He was here to work. Just like the doctors treating his sister. "Please." He held out a hand to the poor frightened nurse and, with an apology, said, "Lead the way."

When he went to see his sister in the observation bay of the secure unit and found Avery there as well, he forced himself to click into "Carter Booth Departure" mode.

"Hey, Cass." He sat down on a stool on the other side of the bed in sync with Avery standing up.

"Don't be rude," Cassidy weakly chastised. "Say hi to your girlfriend, too."

"Oh, we're—" he began.

Avery waved her hands and said, "It's okay. I was leaving anyway."

He didn't protest.

He felt his sister poke him in the arm. "You're more of an idiot than I thought you were if you're letting her walk away like that."

He couldn't disagree. He was an idiot for a lot of reasons. He pulled her chart up on his tablet, doing his best to ignore the fact her tiny little hands were attached to the bed by handcuffs and, in as bright a tone as he could muster, thumbed through the notes and said, "Now, let's see here…"

When Carter finally came out of his sister's room, Avery was fuming. How dare he give up on them like that! Yes, he'd warned her that he'd be leaving one day, but nothing had prepared her for the way he'd looked at her

when he'd walked in the room and seen her
with Cassidy.

He didn't even look like Carter—that confident, sexy, cheeky man she'd met on New
Year's Eve. The one who'd bet her a kiss he
could ride a bull longer than she did.

It made her heart physically ache to see him
like this. Slump-shouldered. Bearing the weight
of the inevitable. But it *wasn't* inevitable. Cassidy had already said she wanted Carter to have
girlfriends. She'd just finished telling Avery
that she had begged Carter for years to quit his
hovering. So really, Carter was the only one
denying Carter a girlfriend. And as much as
she ached for him, she hurt for herself, as well.

Carter looked shocked to see Avery, but he
set a pace that meant only one thing: *I'm moving on.* "I thought you'd be long—"

She cut him off. "I know what you thought."

Carter laughed, but he did not sound amused.
"What are saying, Avery? That you're surprised
things turned out exactly like I told you they
would?"

"No," she ground out. "I'm surprised that a
man as strong as you are can't find a way to
let himself be loved by his sister and by someone else. By me."

There. It was out there now. The fact that
she loved him.

His lips moved as if he were going to say something in return but thought better of it.

"What do you think is going to happen if you let yourself fall in love with me, Carter?" Again, he didn't answer, so she persisted. "Your sister isn't going to die because you find love. You know that, right? If anything, she might be happy for you. Maybe she'd even see it as an example. Something to aspire toward."

He gritted his teeth, a muscle in his jaw twitching as he did. "You don't know what it's like."

She laughed at that one. "Really? I don't know what it's like to have someone I love with all my heart get sick and know that one day, no matter what I do, they're going to die? C'mon, Carter. You're better than that. I know *exactly* what it's like. Only your sister…she's alive! So why don't you celebrate that by giving her a brother who's happy?"

"If you're so smart, how about you explain why building a shrine to your dead sister was such a good idea?"

Avery goldfished for a minute. If he'd physically struck her, it would've hurt less. "You know why I bought that house. And you helped me do it."

He shook his head. "I only gave you the reasons you wanted to justify buying it."

Her breath was coming in short painful huffs now. She knew everything he was saying was coming from a place of fear. Of hurt and a deep well of grief that this might be the time his sister finally lost her battle for survival. She got that. But she'd been through that exact same journey and Carter was the man who'd helped her see things from the other side. The one who'd helped her realize that life wasn't made up of just one single thread. It was composed of all sorts of threads. Beautiful ones. Painful ones. Loving ones. Ones like this that hurt so bad it was almost impossible to bear, but all those threads made a person stronger. And she wanted to be stronger, not weaker. If Carter left now, she knew she'd have lost one of the key threads that had helped put her back together. And that, even though he wouldn't admit it, he had, too.

He kept on walking and yanked a door open to the stairwell. She followed.

A desperation clawed at her, a visceral need to get him to see that the way he was living wasn't working anymore.

Carter didn't stop climbing stairs until they reached the roof level. Mercifully, it was free of any other medical personnel. He looked out into the middle distance, but she could tell he was listening.

"Okay, Carter. Tell me. What if you do leave now, huh? What happens when you follow Cassidy from this hospital to the next one and the next one after that? At some point, it's going to take her, Carter. You know that better than most. And what are you going to do, then? What's your reason for living going to be once that sweet girl in there can't fight anymore?"

It was a blunt way to put it, but she felt she had to say it. She'd made the mistake of putting her own life on hold during April's illness. She'd lost a perfectly nice boyfriend. Some friends. And now her family. She'd hate for Carter to endure the same heartache she had. Or, more accurately, the numbness.

He crossed his arms over his chest. "If you're so wise, why don't you illuminate me? Tell me what *your* reason for living was after April died?"

You.

She couldn't make herself say it. She knew Carter was angry. And scared and hurt and plain old pissed off at life, but it was hard receiving these point-blank blows. Each word hitting like a real bullet.

Carter's eyes snagged with hers and held. She'd never felt pain looking into them before but this time she did. She felt his pain. His anguish. But she didn't hear the one thing she was hoping for. An admission that he loved her, too.

She tried to reason with him, but it felt like she was begging for her own life. "Look. I know you're mad at the world, but have you ever considered that Cassidy might need to make her own mistakes? Scratch her knees. Bruise her elbows. Figure out how to pick herself up?"

"No." He cut her off. "Listen, Avery. I told you this was how I operated. That this is how I deal with things." He looked away for a minute—as if he were having a proper fistfight with his emotions—only continuing once he'd pummeled them into submission. "I know it's not a perfect way to live, and believe me, I wish like hell things were different. But they're not." He pointed to the hospital beneath them. "That woman in there—Cassidy—is my only family. She is sick and I promised her daddy—*my* daddy—that I would do everything I could to look after her. I don't have the big pools of emotional resources you obviously do. I wasn't raised by people who made me feel safe and secure. The only thing I know is loss. So, yeah. You win. Your heart is bigger. Your spirit is kinder. I wish I'd been built the same way, but I wasn't. I'm sorry that it has to be like this, but it does."

She tried to protest, to tell him it wasn't a contest over who had bigger emotional reserves, but he cut her off. "I've got to go. I'm sorry, Avery. I truly am."

It felt almost impossible to watch him walk away, but she knew she had to. Carter said Cassidy was all the family he had. He wasn't allowing himself to believe he could build one of his own with her. She was shivering but going into the warm heat of the hospital just seemed wrong. She wanted her body to feel the way her heart did. Growing so cold it would eventually be numb to the pain.

CHAPTER FOURTEEN

AVERY SENT LIA a text agreeing to meet at their *special spot*, even though she wasn't in the mood to be inspired or have her spirits lifted. She was back in "work is where I shut everything out" mode and was quite happy wallowing in it, thank you very much. But she loved her friend, so…she went.

Whereas most of the doctors and nurses she knew met outside the new babies unit for a bit of an *aw* moment, she and Lia had a different kind of happy. The physio ward. St. Dolly's had received a massive trust from a famous actor who'd fallen off his horse a few years back and had been paralyzed. The hospital had used the money to build a state of the art physio unit that looked more like an Olympic training gym than anything, until you actually started paying attention to who was doing the work and why they were doing it.

Avery went up to the second level of the unit

and looked down at the patients. Some were having to learn how to walk from scratch, how to function without a limb, how to live the rest of their adult lives in a wheelchair.

For forty-eight entire hours, she'd been trying to teach herself how to live without Carter Booth.

After his sister had been discharged, he'd "discharged" himself from the roster. Disappeared from her house as if he'd never been there. Disappeared from her life.

It had been awful. Like watching someone flick a switch on their emotions. One minute, you thought they loved you. The next…you felt as if you'd imagined it all.

His departure made her body feel as if everything alive in it had been replaced by an empty void. She'd fallen for Carter. Hook, line and sinker. Let herself believe what she had felt for him was exactly what he had felt for her. True love.

She'd been kidding herself when she'd believed what they'd shared could override a lifetime of packing his bags and walking away. Getting herself to understand that had felt like swallowing shards of glass.

Lia had gently pointed out that Carter compartmentalized his life in order to survive. Just like she did.

Avery got that. He'd not had an easy life, but it still hurt to know he'd shut the door on her without so much as a backward glance. Locked it and thrown away the key for all she knew.

She could find out. She still had his number. But she also had her pride. They'd made a deal and what little self-worth she had right now she was keeping close. And, yes. She knew deep down that pride was a stupid thing to cling to when she was standing here on two perfectly serviceable feet, watching people confronting much greater challenges than a broken heart. She saw the pain on their faces. The sweat on their brows. Heard their cries of agony as their bodies refused to do what they once did with ease. This was why she didn't go to the baby ward. Their lives were shiny and new. Beautiful blank spaces upon which entire collages of discovery had yet to be drawn.

Hers was a slate that couldn't be wiped clean. She bore the scars of her sister's death and now Carter's departure, as if they were actual physical wounds. But…

She forced herself to rein in the pity party. Even though she didn't have Carter Booth to hold her in his arms at night, she still had her body and her health.

"Hey, you." Lia slid her forearms onto the

railing Avery was leaning on. "Are we talking today or just watching?"

"Bit of both." Avery's voice wobbled. When they'd met yesterday, she hadn't been able to talk. Not a word.

But she'd showed Lia the note Carter had left. The one that said he wasn't very good with words, so he was going to borrow a few from a mutual heroine of theirs. Dolly Parton. There was a particular song that spoke to him. One called "I Will Always Love You." He knew he hadn't told her in as many words, but the song covered the gamut of how he felt.

He'd quoted the lyrics that made it clear they weren't meant to be together, but that their time together would always be cherished. She knew her takeaway from his message should be happiness that he had, in his own way, loved her. But how was that going to help her pick up the pieces of her heart and start again? Knowing that she had been loved but hadn't been enough to stay for? Fight for?

They watched in silence for a few minutes until Lia twisted her torso so that she was facing Avery. "Deena wanted me to have a word with you about the concert."

Avery's tongue hit the roof of her mouth in preparation to say, *No way*, when she remembered the promise she'd made was to Bonnie, not to Carter. The vow was to sing for her sister and all the other people who would have to take the same journeys she and April had. Journeys of love and loss. She supposed she never would've been out and about on a New Year's Eve, riding a mechanical bull to earn the money to buy Five Acre Farm if April had lived. They would've been making music somewhere. Watching someone else make it. Or, perhaps, tucked up on a sofa, watching a box set, assuring one another they weren't boring, they were prudent. Saving yet more precious pennies for their house. But the truth was with the jobs they'd had and the money they'd saved… they could have bought Five Acre Farm years ago.

Her mind rattled back through countless memories with her sister. One thing she'd always known, but never acknowledged, became abundantly clear. Avery was the leather to her sister's lace. The country to April's rock 'n' roll. Avery loved horses and the smell of grass after rainfall and country lanes. April loved the heart of Nashville, clothes weighted with rhinestones and the limelight. And boy did she shine when she was in it.

She saw it now as if it were on a billboard for all to see. Her sister had made her feel whole because of their differences rather than their similarities.

As clear as the hand in front of her face, Avery knew April went along with Avery's dreams about Five Acre to make her happy. As such, she owed her sister a concert. One that honored her memory. Celebrated it.

Her heart softened. Though she missed him deeply, wanted him here more than she could ever say, she owed Carter her gratitude for getting her here, to this place, where she believed in herself enough to get up on stage and sing about love again. About heartache. And all the lessons life taught you whether or not you wanted to learn them.

She sent a sheepish smile to Lia. "I think I need to find some musicians."

Lia grinned and pulled her into a tight hug. "You sure?"

Avery gave a nervous giggle. "No. But I've got to start somewhere, right? Remember what April always said?"

In unison, they both said, "Go big or go home!"

Lia pointed at Avery's heart. "Do we need to meet for a Guac and Talk later? Drink some sorrow juice?"

Tears welled in her eyes, but she shook her head no. Even a sip of a margarita would start her ugly crying and admitting that Carter had broken her heart.

She understood why he'd made the choice he had. But it was still a raw wound and the only way she wanted to deal with it right now was to focus on something else. Give her pain some space to do what it needed to in order to heal. It had taken nearly two years of actively mourning her sister to sing again. Less than two months for Carter to gallop into her life, her heart and shake it all up like a snow globe, reminding her that nothing was permanent. No matter how much you tried to hold on to it. The best thing to do was offer gratitude for the good parts and learn from the bad ones. Like losing her sister, she'd need more than two days to get over Carter, but she'd get there, because as painful as it felt right now, she knew there'd come a day when she could look back on their time together with a smile. Bittersweet memories, indeed.

A tissue box hurtling across the room was Carter's greeting from his sister.

Arms held up in front of his face in case there were more missiles coming his way he asked, "What the hell was that for?"

Though she was still bedridden with fatigue, Cassidy had steam coming out of her ears. "Carter Booth, can you please explain to me exactly how you became a doctor with so few brain cells knocking around that head of yours?"

"What are you talking about?"

"How'd you even find out where I was, let alone get a job here?"

He scrubbed his jaw. Telling her might not be the wisest course of action. Being a doctor in a prison hospital wasn't exactly in the choice pickings department, so that had been easy enough to get. As for finding her... That had been the hard part.

After she'd been discharged from St. Dolly's without his knowledge, he'd called in every favor he'd ever been owed and come up with nothing. In the end, he'd driven down to the barbecue joint where a lot of paramedics hung out and pretty much begged them to tell him where Cassidy was. Somehow, she'd ended up at the Women's Correctional Facility here on the outskirts of Louisville, Kentucky.

"Dumb luck," he finally said.

"Dumb is about right," his sister agreed.

"What are you all het up for anyway? You should be resting."

She glared at him, then at the hospital ward she was in. "You just don't get it, do you?"

"Get what?"

"You should be with that amazing girlfriend you stupidly left behind in Nashville, Carter. Leave. Me. Alone."

He felt the words like knives. "But... I'm your brother."

She saw the hurt she'd caused and softened. "I know that, you bozo. I love you. But isn't it about time you had a life of your own?"

"I do have a life. With you."

"No, Carter." She took his hand and pressed it to her pale cheek before weaving her fingers in with his. "You don't. From the sounds of things, you were just beginning to have a life with Avery and, yet again, you threw it away to chase me around the country." She pursed her lips at him. "You've got to back off. Focus on your own stupid mistakes. I'm great at making my own, and it is high time I started putting together a toolkit to be able to fix them."

Carter could almost hear Avery's voice in his ear. The one that had told him he needed to back off. She wasn't the type to say I told you so, but she would've earned it this time around.

Cassidy was still glaring at him. "Carter. You've got to start seeing what I do."

"What are you even talking about, Cass?"

She huffed out an exasperated sigh as if he really were thick as two short planks. "Knowing you're always around to pick up the pieces of my life has made me reckless. Too reckless."

He was about to say amen to that when he realized that she really meant it. He got up, yanked the curtains around her bed closed and propped himself up on the end of it. "Talk to me."

And she did. She told him about how the longer sentence had put her in a section of the prison that really opened up her eyes to what she'd done. She was surrounded by women who'd made bad decisions that had years' long ramifications. For the first time in her life, she felt lonely. And no, that didn't mean she wanted him to visit more. It meant she needed to work out how to turn her life around. Spend more time with people like her cellmate back in Nashville.

"Why her?" Carter asked.

"She was the one who convinced me to go to the AA meetings. I went just to get her to shut up at first. But then some of the things they were saying started to sink in. One of them in particular."

"What was it?"

Cassidy's lips did a little twitch, as if she were fighting off some unwanted emotion, but she persisted. "There was a woman in there who'd killed a child when she'd been drunk driving."

Carter frowned.

"That could've been me, Carter," Cassidy said with a gravity he'd not heard from her before. "Behind that wheel. Hitting that child. Taking a life."

He gave a sober nod. It could've been.

"I have no right to take anyone's life and realizing that made me see that another thing I didn't have a right to do was take the life I've been given for granted."

He blinked, trying to absorb what his sister was saying. Was she finally understanding that each minute she had was precious, and as such should be cherished, not frittered away on misguided adrenaline rushes? "If this cellmate of yours was so great, why did you ask for a transfer?"

She frowned at him. "That's now how prison works, big brother. You get taken where you're taken and now that I've decided to start growing up, I'm going to learn from it. I'll go to the AA meetings here. Maybe take a bit more time in their chapel. They've got a real nice one. And maybe see about signing up for some sort of course. They've got me potentially for the next three years, so instead of fighting it like I usually do, maybe it's time to start learning from it.

Take advantage of the good things they have." With a twinkle in her eyes she added, "After all, this is a *correctional* institute."

He gave her hand a squeeze. "Wise words from a little sister."

She grinned and, to his surprise, blushed with pleasure. "Want some more wise words?"

"Sure."

"Go back to Nashville and win back Avery."

Now it was his turn to backpedal. "Aw, now what Avery and I had was a temporary thing." In other words, he was pretty sure he'd screwed that opportunity up. Big time.

Cassidy scoffed, "The way you two looked at each other? I'm calling bull!"

Carter feigned being wounded in his chest and then, when he saw she really meant it, he let her words soak in. Hands clasped over his chest; his brain finally connected with his heart. It was Cupid's arrow stuck in there. Not a knife.

Cassidy was right. He was in love with Avery and like a class A idiot, he'd pulled the plug on it without even having an adult conversation with her. He'd basically had a one-way shouting match with her, refusing to genuinely listen to what she was trying to say to him. When remorse had hit for being such a jackass, he'd let the lyrics of a country song do his apologizing for him. And it hadn't even been that. It had been a get-out clause.

Cassidy was right. He *was* being stupid. He loved Avery. Had from the second he'd laid eyes on her. And he owed it to her to tell her how he really felt.

He would always love her. And he wanted to keep on loving her, up close and personal.

More than that, to be the man he knew deep down he could be. One who was reliable. Loving. Wanted a family. Hell. The whole nine yards. He wanted a diamond wedding anniversary with one woman and one woman only. Avery Whittacker.

And Cassidy was right. Avery, too. There were no laws preventing him from driving up to Louisville to see his sister. A city where there were big hospitals with smart doctors who knew all about sickle cell anemia. Doctors who'd taken oaths to care and protect, just as he had. He swore under his breath.

Despite the very real possibility that he'd ruined his chances of Avery loving him in return, he was going to have to try. Even if he made a fool out of himself doing it.

"What?" Cassidy demanded. "What are you shaking your head for?"

"I'm like the worst kind of country song."

"What do you mean?"

"The kind where the singer had the girl of his dreams and let her slip through his fingers because he was stupid."

"I told you that you were stupid." Cassidy looked smug, but also concerned for him.

Carter rose and gave her a little tip of an imaginary Stetson. "It looks like it's about time I started taking advice from my very wise kid sister."

Cassidy clapped her hands. "You going to go all out? Buy the ring? Get the roses?"

Carter had no idea what he was going to do. "I've got a six-hour drive to think about it."

Cassidy gave him a satisfied grin. "Go on, then. Shoo." She flicked her fingers. "Get her back. Clock's a ticking! And bring her next time you come calling. Visiting hour's much more fun with her than you."

"Thanks a lot!" Carter gave her a wounded look, but Cassidy had hit the nail on the head again. It wasn't just visiting hour that was better with Avery. It was everything that was better with Avery.

CHAPTER FIFTEEN

AVERY WAS ABSOLUTELY EXHAUSTED. She'd just pulled a double shift and because it wasn't any fun going home to a house without Carter in it, she'd slept at Lia's and pulled another double. Probably not the winning recipe for sounding her best when she sang at the concert tomorrow night, but a raspy voice worked for Miley, so she hoped it would work for her, too.

When she pulled her car into the drive, she heaved out a heavy sigh. She'd have to get used to walking in here and feeling her own energy fill the place. Not look at all of that space that had been created when Carter packed his bags and headed for heaven knew where.

She forced herself out of the car and, allowing herself just a tiny pity party, stomped up the steps, across the porch and stuffed her key in the lock.

When she pushed the door open, she froze. She hadn't left any table lamps on. Mostly because she didn't own any. She certainly hadn't lit any candles. Or a fire. And she definitely hadn't laid out a thick trail of rose petals that, now that her eyes were focusing, she could see were shaped into an arrow pointing at the stairs…also covered in rose petals.

The table saw was gone. As were the rest of carpentry items the builders had left lying around the living room. In fact, it was all looking really good. Not a bit like the shambles she'd left when she decided she needed some space from Five Acre while she decided whether to keep it or chalk the purchase up to a "good lesson learned" and move on. Before her brain could entirely put the pieces of this very romantic-looking puzzle together… Carter appeared at the top of the stairwell, guitar slung over his shoulder, fingers strumming a tune. And then he began to sing.

He was right. He was an awful singer, but the words he'd written filled her heart with so much joy she would've listened to him forever.

He loved her.

He'd made a bad call. The wrong one. He had never met a woman who'd compelled him to examine how healthy his relationship with his sister was. Whether it did either of them any good. But his sister had set him straight, then turned him around and now here he was, heart on his sleeve, hoping like hell he could make things right. He'd work all day and strum all night if he needed to, but mostly he wanted to spend the rest of his life with her by his side.

"Avery," he sang as he lowered himself to one knee, "you make my voice wavery."

Avery started giggling. Giggling and crying and running up the stairs to him because the space between them was too big and she needed to close it and kiss him and smell him and feel his arms around her again because every pore in her body had ached for him since he'd left. He unclipped the guitar and before he could sing another lyric, they were kissing. Hot, hungry love-filled kisses that only held promises of more to come rather than the bittersweet ache that this was all going to come to an end.

When they surfaced for air, Carter asked, "Can I take it you accept my apology?"

Avery grinned. "You can. I suppose we should talk about exactly what it is you want, though. From us."

"I want all of it," he said. He dug around in his pocket and pulled out a little box. The kind that only held one type of thing.

Her heart flew into her throat as he flicked the box open and revealed a beautiful ring unlike anything she'd ever seen. It had to have been handmade. The band was made of a beautiful warm rose gold, but not in a traditional smooth band with a diamond solitaire. The band looked like tiny flower stems woven together and, as he held it out for her to inspect, she knew there was no other man in the world who would know her well enough to choose this exact ring. There were tiny little gold roses and leaves elegantly binding a trio of basket settings holding three beautiful lavender-colored sapphires in place. It was a country girl's ring. One that she absolutely knew she did not have the power to refuse. Nor did she want to. And he must've seen the answer in her eyes, because before she could put a voice to anything, he readjusted himself so that he was propped back up in the kneeling position. Even though she was sitting on the floor across from him, the gesture felt like he was laying down all the armor he'd worn around his heart for her. This was him in his purest form. Putting his trust in her. His love.

"Avery Whittacker, this may not be exactly the proposal you wanted. I know I'm a frog who comes with a lot of warts, but I promise to do my best by you. My very best. I made myself believe Cassidy was my only family, but of all the people in the world, she's the one who reminded me family were the people you loved. And I love you. I will make mistakes. I will do my best to learn from them. I will never have your beautiful songbird voice, but I promise to accompany you on this life journey to the fullest of my ability. To make you as happy as you make me. Will you let me be your wingman?"

Avery shook her head. "No. Absolutely not." She couldn't bear the stricken look on his face, so quickly finished the sentence. "I want you to be my copilot."

He needn't have bothered with the Tiffany lamps and jam jars filled with candles. His smile was enough to light up the entire house. He whooped and slipped the ring on her finger, and the next thing she knew, Avery was in his arms being whirled around and around with his lips pressed to hers. When they finally came to a stop, Avery saw that they were outside the bedroom. She grimaced. "I'm really sorry, but I haven't been much of a housekeeper lately. I haven't been home for a few days."

"I know," he said, his lips twitching with a mischievous smile.

"You never gave me back the key I gave you, did you?" She grinned because it wasn't like his having access to the house had been a bad thing.

"No, I gave that back. But I might have remembered the spare key beneath the plant by the back door."

She smacked herself on the forehead. "How long have you been here?"

He tapped the side of his nose. "I heard from a little birdie that you were working hard, so I thought I'd put a bit of extra effort into the first time I saw you again rather than appear all straggly and lovelorn and miserable."

She wrapped her arms around his waist and tilted her chin up so she could look into his beautiful green eyes. "You were straggly, lovelorn and miserable without me?"

"Bereft." And then, more seriously, he said, "I was. And I never should have done that. Not listened to you. Walked away angry. If you want me to apologize until the end of time for my behavior, I will."

"No," she said, placing a soft kiss on his lips. "As much as it hurt—it was a good thing."

His eyebrows dove together. "Why?"

She looked away, then realized she owed him as much honesty as he'd shown her. "I think it gave me some perspective on losing my sister."

"In what way?"

"I will always miss her. There is no doubt about that, but I think I went so far inside myself to grieve her loss, I forgot to acknowledge the whole April. The one who would definitely not have wanted me to put my life on ice because she wasn't here anymore."

Carter dropped a kiss on her forehead. "From everything I've heard about her, that sounds about right."

Avery nodded. Then shook her head. "When she got sick, it was like my brain stopped working. All that mattered was caring for her. Making sure every second she had left was precious. I hate that I lost her. And God knows I would've done anything to keep her alive, but that's not how life works. It gives. It takes. And you have to cherish the moments you do have, not regret the ones you never will."

"Sounds like a country song in the making." Carter swept his fingertips along her jawline as she smiled.

"It does, doesn't it?" She grinned. "See! That's what I was saying. Realizing that about April made me understand that loving you was better than not having known that sort of love at all."

He ran his hands down her back and tugged her in close. "I hope this isn't the part where you tell me I can hop on my horse and leave town again."

"Not a chance, Carter Booth. You're all mine!" She kissed him, then pulled back again. "I guess I also needed to realize that love is something that takes all forms. Even frogs with warts," she added with a cheeky wink.

"I'll show you a frog with warts!" He laughed and scooped her up into his arms, then pushed the bedroom door open.

Avery gasped in delight. In place of the air mattress and the mountain of sleeping bags and quilts, was her dream bedroom. Even though it was night, it felt light and airy thanks to the beautiful soft lighting and gorgeous wallpaper covered in tiny little wildflowers. There were upcycled bedside tables and, though she'd only mentioned it in passing, a hope chest at the foot of the bed and a rocking chair by the window. "Did you do all this?"

"Yes, ma'am," he said, gently placing her down on the huge sleigh bed. "Me and the contractors."

"It's amazing!" And it was. Exactly what she'd dreamed of when she thought of spending the night wrapped in her true love's arms.

"Now," Carter sat down beside her, his fingers teasing at the top button of her blouse, "if I'm right, that tiny bird who I've been in touch with down at the hospital says you need to get some shut-eye before your big night tomorrow."

Avery gave him a doe-eyed blink of innocence. "That's true. But I can think of one thing I'd like to do before that."

"Oh?"

"Yes. Practice with my guitar player."

She didn't need to explain exactly what it was she wanted to practice, because Carter knew precisely what she meant. He swiftly began undoing each and every button that stood between them. Making love that night was sweeter than all the times they'd been together before, because this time, with a ring on her finger and a promise in both of their hearts, she felt loved. A "forever and always" kind of love. Exactly the kind the country stars liked to make folk think was unattainable. But she knew it wasn't. You had to find the right guy, work hard at really getting to know one another and then spend the rest of your life making sure he knows you love him. Which was precisely what she planned on doing.

"You ready?" Carter felt more nervous than Avery looked. In fact, she didn't look nervous at all. "There are hundreds of people out there. Don't you feel even a little bit of the jitters?"

"Not with my man by my side."

He grinned and couldn't stop himself from crooking a finger underneath her chin and pulling her in close for a last kiss before they went on stage.

"You're happy with all the songs you picked?"

Avery nodded, enjoying the glints and sparks that occurred each time the stage lights caught glimpses of her engagement ring even from here in the wings. "I picked a half-and-half set."

"What do you mean?"

"Half the songs are ones I know April loved singing."

He nodded his approval. He loved seeing this strength in her. The power that could fuel her love for her sister and the times they shared versus drain and weaken her in the wake of her loss. It was an important lesson to learn. To think he'd almost opted to feel that same pain, that same weakness, made him realize how lucky he was to have a sister who, despite her faults, had enough common sense to call a spade a spade. He'd been stupid, and she hadn't been shy in letting him know.

"What are the other half?"

She grinned and flushed a little. "Love songs."

"Oh, yeah? Now what would make you want to sing love songs all night?"

She ramped up the coquette in her hips and gave him a saucy little swish and turn before saying, "It's Valentine's Day."

"That all?"

"Hmm…" She looked down at her hand, then back up at him, unable to contain her grin anymore. "That. And I just got engaged to the man of my dreams."

"He must be one lucky guy."

"Oh, he is," she assured him. "And I am a very, very happy bride-to-be."

"How happy are you?"

"Want me to show you?"

He lifted his chin. He sure did, but he also had to walk on stage and not embarrass himself in less than a minute, so he said, "How about you show me after we do this little sing song?"

"Here's a teaser." Avery leaned in and gave him a kiss that was sweeter than a perfect peach. It was a nice taste to have on his lips as they were called closer to the stage to prepare for their set. He saw the light catch on Avery's ring and her goofy smile when she noticed it, too.

Buying that ring and putting it on her finger was one of the smartest things he'd ever done. A new start. A chance to provide the type of love and care to a woman—his woman—that he'd never imagined possible. But here he was, living the dream.

The act that was on stage finished up their

set and before he knew it, he and Avery were walking side by side onto the stage to rapturous applause. He knew it wasn't for him. It was for Avery. But he basked in the glow because the only person she had eyes for as she began her first song, a love song, was him.

* * * * *

*Look out for the next story in the
Nashville ER duet*

Their Reunion to Remember
by Tina Beckett

*If you enjoyed this story, check out these
other great reads from Annie O'Neil*

The Princess and the Pediatrician
Hawaiian Medic to Rescue His Heart
A Family Made in Rome

All available now!